To Ashley

Read to your Dragon every Night

Diana Metz

# TALON AND THE DRAGONS OF CRINNELIA

DIANA METZ

The M.O.T.H.E.R. Publishing Co., Inc.
PO Box 477
Rock Springs, WY 82902
www.motherpublishing.com

Published 2002 by The M.O.T.H.E.R. Publishing Co., Inc.



Inquiries should be addressed to:
The M.O.T.H.E.R. Publishing Co., Inc.
PO Box 477
Rock Springs, WY 82902-0477
www.motherpublishing.com

First paperback edition 2002

Summary: A young man's life is changed when he encounters a wizard and befriends a dragon.

ISBN 0-9718431-1-2

Library of Congress Control Number: 2002094676

1. Dragons – Fiction. 2. Wizards – Fiction. 3. Magic – Fiction I. Title

Printed in the United States of America

Many Thanks

To Dave, for everything
To Michael, for inspiration
To Brian, for giving me a reason to write
To Anna, who let me know if I did it right
To my parents, who gave me a fantastic childhood
To Janet, who knows where all the *that*s went

*****

"We've been out here all morning, Tolago. I think you're lost." The large yellow dragon wove lazily through the clouds.

"I am not. I remember flying over that mountain, we go over that way." The sounds of battle could soon be heard on the wind. "Hear that, I told you."

"Yeah, yeah, so there's a war going on, what else is new?" Felgrig felt hungry, and tired. Tolago had dragged him on this wild goose chase just as his guard duty had ended and he hadn't had a chance to grab a bite to eat, not even a wild goose.

"There's something odd down there, I tell you. I flew by and got a strange feeling. When I got closer it hit me like a thunder bolt."

"Probably indigestion," Felgrig mumbled to himself.

The sounds of battle grew louder, and soon the landscape of war was spread out before them. The wind carried the smell of newly spilled blood. Felgrig's stomach rumbled. His mouth watered. He began descending.

Tolago stopped him. "That's not what we're here for. Control yourself."

Felgrig glared at his friend. "Don't blame *me*; you're the one that insisted that I skip breakfast to follow you out here." Felgrig sighed.

As the two drew closer to the center of the battlefield Felgrig began to feel an odd hum in his head. Past the main fighting and closer to the battle standards a strong vibration hit him.

Tolago turned to his friend, "You feel it, don't you."

Felgrig didn't notice the I-told-you-so tone in Tolago's voice. "A wizard?"

"I don't think so. It's too white for one of *them*. But just to be sure, let's get closer." Tolago moved closer in.

Felgrig followed. Maybe he could snatch a quick bite before Tolago noticed.

They circled lower, searching for the source of the unusual vibration.

"It's one of those, by the ridge."

"The fat one?"

"Stop thinking with your stomach, Felgrig. No, that small one, with all those dead around it."

"It's awfully good with that sword." Felgrig noted.

"But is that all?" Tolago asked. "Watch it closely, it anticipates the adversaries next move, it's very cunning."

Felgrig had to agree with his companion. "But it's so young," there was a note of awe in his voice. "You're right; its essence is too clean to be a wizard."

Tolago inhaled deeply. "It doesn't even *smell* like one of them."

“There’s no doubt that it’s using magic.” Felgrig tilted his head in thought. “But if it’s not a wizard, what is it?”

“We should kill it! Kill it now, while it’s young!”

Felgrig was taken aback at the hatred he heard in his friend’s voice. “Calm down. This may be bigger than we think. If it’s this powerful it may have powerful friends. We don’t want to start something on our own. We should tell the Matriarch about this.” Felgrig rose high into the air. “And on the way back we can get some breakfast. All this fresh meat makes me hungry.”

Tolago hesitated, and grudgingly followed. “Ok, we’ll do it your way.” He looked back at the shrinking landscape below. “I guess we can always find it later if She decides it must be destroyed. Just remember, I was the one who found it first.”

*****

## Chapter 1

Talon sat high on his horse. His sword hung at his side. He felt tired beyond exhaustion. The sun and the weight of his armor had taken their toll. The idea of leaving the battlefield in full armor had been an egotistical one, and a full day's ride had beaten his pride to a pulp. This was surely not helping his battle-bruised limbs. His helmet, now bumping on the horse's rump, had been removed earlier, allowing the breeze to dry the sweat from the short-trimmed black hair. The hard, cold eyes seemed out of place in the boyish face. Dust and dried blood did not hide the lack of beard on the soft cheeks.

The road became congested at Arklin's gates. News of the battle's end had traveled fast. As Talon rode up to the battered gates he noticed that the guards were not armed, another sign that words travel faster than horses.

Arklin looked like a dozen other villages lining the Trade Road. Ten or so two-story buildings were widely spaced on either side of a rutted dirt street. People competed with horses and wagons along the street, as well as dogs, goats, chickens and the occasional pig. Street vendors shouted above all the noise to catch the attention of passersby. Faded wood signs swung noisily above storefronts. Talon knew these bustling streets had been deserted only the day before with the windows boarded up against the possibility that the Duke's war would spill into the town. Shops were now filled with patrons who had been afraid to leave their farms.

Talon located the stables at the edge of town. He dismounted and pulled off his saddlebag. He gave his horse a pat and scratched its ear. "Time for a rest boy, for both of us." A weary stableboy led the horse into the stable.

Talon slung the saddlebags over one shoulder and walked into town. The dry dirt street muffled the sound of Talon's armored boots. He was oblivious of his surroundings; one town looked much like another. The townsfolk were equally oblivious of Talon; one soldier looked much like another, and there were plenty of them in town this evening.

The local inn was easily found; the noise from its tavern filled the street. After securing a room and changing out of his armor, Talon went in search of a hot meal. When he stepped into the crowded tavern several of his fellow soldiers acknowledged him. But they did not ask Talon to join their table. Talon was not part of their group. It was not his youth that separated him, but his abilities. At fifteen, Talon was ten years younger than most of the men he fought beside, though he was far superior as swordsman. He parried and thrust at just the right moment to defeat his opponents. Talon also had an uncanny ability to know where and when the enemy would attack. This elevated him quickly through the ranks to Lead Strategist of Count Elanza's army. This did not sit well with many of the generals. His fellow soldiers appreciated his talents, but were suspicious of them as well. So Talon sat alone in the dark isolated corner. The barmaid brought him a mug of mulled cider.

A deep swallow of the warm, spiced drink helped to ease the tension of the day. The jovial atmosphere around him could not relieve the sense of emptiness he felt. The tedious, petty war between Count Elanza and Duke Nidral had occupied Talon's life for the past year. It had only been settled when Duke Nidral's son had come to the realization that his future workforce was being cut to ribbons. With a little cutting of his own, the son inherited the family title and quickly ended the war. The count disbanded his army and Talon was now out of a job.

The war earnings Talon had been given would only support him for a few months and he was uncertain where he would go from here. There was no place for him at home, his father had been very clear about his objections to Talon's choice to train as a soldier rather than apprentice to a tradesman in town. He had no interest in finding work in a town like Arklin. His brilliance as a tactician could secure him a post in any army, but his taste for war had soured and he knew that he didn't want to spend his life moving from battle to battle. Was there anything else ahead for him? He sighed heavily.

"Life can't be that grim."

Talon pulled his knife, surprised at being caught unaware. An old man sat down in the empty chair across the table. He had neither the look of a traveler nor thief. Perhaps a beggar, his ragged clothes and unwashed appearance pointed in that direction. But he was too bold, and his bright blue eyes belied a destitute lifestyle. Just one of the townsfolk, he looked harmless enough; Talon laid the knife on the table and leaned over his mug. "Go away, old man; I'm in no mood for conversation."

"No?" A grin spread lines and furrows across the ancient face. "You seem to be the only one here tonight who isn't. I haven't heard this many war stories since the Earl of Chancely led his assault on Dalvian mines. A thousand of Chancely's men were lost in the endless caverns. The Dalvians hid in the mud and ambushed the unwitting soldiers. It was rather ingenious of Chancely to flood the mines. I heard that the gold they removed later filled fifty wagons. Not since then has a war-prize been so high. A full purse seems to bring out the storyteller in your breed."

Talon grunted.

"Quiet type, huh? I like that. Blood and dismemberment doesn't appeal to me as much as it used to, and one despot is much like another after a few centuries. Now a well-plotted intrigue, that makes for interesting conversation. I could talk to a spy for hours, and a talkative chambermaid is a wealth of scandalous stories. Barbers, now there's someone who could talk for hours---"

"How could he ever get a word in? You haven't taken a breath since you sat down." Talon drained his mug and waved for the barmaid to bring him another.

"I tend to do that, you know. I don't get out as much as I should, and the chance of getting some decent human contact tends to bring out the chatter. Not that I mind being left alone, no. Used to be a time when I couldn't get a minute of peace, people dropping by at all hours, no consideration about privacy or property. Just walk right in. Demanding, and pleading, wanting me to fix this or cure that, couldn't get a decent night's sleep. No consideration at all. Why, I once had a whole family camp out on my doorstep, and they wouldn't leave until I cured the baby of whooping croup. Then one day some farmer got a run of bad luck, you know; drought, locust, horse went lame, wife gave birth to triplet girls, that sort of thing -- well it all got blamed on me. Had to leave town. Found a nice spot up in the woods though, nice and quiet. I don't seem to have any trouble sleeping any more, nod off at the drop of a hat, now. Why just last night..."

"Find someone else to bore with your stories, old man, I'm not interested." Talon turned away from the table.

The old man seemed unflustered, "A bit cynical for your age, aren't you? When did they start using babes in battle?" Before Talon could defend himself the old man stood up. "Well, when you get a break in your important schedule, and you're ready for a new job, you might be interested in this 'boring old man'."

Before Talon knew it, he was alone. "Quick for his age," Talon thought. He noticed a folded piece of paper on the table where his guest had been sitting. Talon picked up the paper and unfolded it. A bright gold coin lay in its center. "All right, now you have my attention." Talon looked at the paper; some directions had been neatly printed on one side. He was tempted to throw the paper in the fire, but he was intrigued. What could the shabby old man want with a young soldier? He stuffed the paper and the coin into a pocket and went up to his room.

The next morning dawned cold and dreary. The prospects for an enjoyable, relaxing day were nonexistent. Talon could find no reason to hang around town and decided to visit the curious old man. He saddled his horse and headed out of town. The dirt road ended abruptly at the edge of a flower filled meadow. It was as if an invisible line had been drawn, saying, "Here, but no further". Talon looked across the meadow and toward the far tree line, and saw no sign of a cottage. There were no signs of a path through the flowers and no smoke from a fireplace. Talon began to think that he had taken a wrong turn.

Once again he looked at the directions he had been given. Urging his horse on, Talon crossed the meadow, found the small brook as described, and followed it to the treeline. Not until he stood directly in front of the trees did Talon see a cave opening. It was so perfectly hidden in the foliage he would have missed it if he hadn't been looking so closely. He was quickly coming to the realization that there was more to the old man than he had thought. Someone only hid when there was something to hide.

Talon tied his horse to a tree, not too close to the entrance of the cave. He wanted to make a quiet entrance. Vines hung down over much of the opening. Talon pulled them back slightly and peered into the darkness. The entrance of the cave was empty, dimly lit by the outside sunlight he let in.

Cautiously, he entered. He paused to let his eyes become accustomed to the darkness.

As Talon walked further into the cave he noticed it didn't have the usual damp, musty feel he expected. It was quite dry and smelled of ginger cakes and fresh cut pine. The floor was well swept, and the stalactites were trimmed close to the ceiling. Talon moved slowly in the dim light.

As he progressed toward the back of the cave, Talon's eyes became used to the darkness. He noticed odd drawings on the walls, swirling geometric shapes, what he assumed was words in some unknown language, and unusual animals. The hair prickled on the back of his neck. This place made him nervous. Talon decided that he didn't want to look too closely at the peculiarly shaped piles along the outer walls, a few were moving. He moved quickly forward. Something brushed his leg and he jumped back, drawing his knife.

A thin line of light could be seen ahead. As he drew closer, Talon saw two blankets on either side of a cavern opening. He peered through. The light made him squint for a moment. Within he saw the old man bent over something on a table, an extraordinarily fat cat was curled on a chair, and a smaller cat wove itself in and out of the man's legs. There was no sign of anyone else in the cave.

"Don't stand there." The voice startled him. "It is perfectly safe, no ambushes, or lurking enemies."

Talon parted the blankets and entered into the room. The old man said nothing else to him, so he filled the silence by looking around. The first peculiarity that struck him was the cavern seemed too large, and he couldn't see the ceiling at all. The fire, which appeared to be the only source of light in the room, could never have given off the amount of light that illuminated the place. Where was the rest of the light coming from? An acrid odor drifted from a large slab workbench where a bowl of green slime bubbled without help from a flame.

A soft rubbing around his boots brought Talon's attention to his feet. The smaller of the two cats had come to greet him. Talon stepped around the ball of fluff toward the old man, who still hadn't turned around. When he came up beside him Talon saw that the old fellow was busily kneading bread dough. Talon took this time to study the old man. He was drawn to the brightness of the old man's eyes; they didn't fit in with the age implied by the white hair and beard. Below the sharp eyes was a long pointy nose that stuck out over a bushy mustache. If a chin could be seen under the long beard, Talon was sure it would rival the sharpness of the nose. Any skin not covered with unkept hair was a maze of fine wrinkles. Talon would have expected a man of such apparent antiquity to be slow moving and dull. But the quickness of the leathery hands in the dough cautioned Talon against making assumptions about this man.

"Well, here I am. Do you have a job for me?" Talon wanted this meeting to be as brief as possible. He was beginning to regret coming at all.

The old man took his time answering. He seemed more concerned about the shape of his loaf. Once he had formed it just right and placed it by the fire, he wiped off his hands and sized up the young man before him. "Aren't you a bit young to be fighting in a war?" The old man poured two mugs of dark warm fluid from a blackened pot and handed one to Talon.

Talon sipped the drink, found it flavorful and took a larger swallow. "How old do you have to be to know injustice when you see it?" The old man didn't look impressed with Talon's answer. "Second sons are expendable and the generals didn't ask for my age."

Picking up the large cat, the old man sat near the fire and motioned for Talon to join him. "Probably wondering what an old man like me would want to hire a soldier for."

Talon shrugged.

"I have a proposition for you. I need someone to go to Precanlin, pick up a package and bring it back." He didn't look at Talon when he spoke, but gazed into the flames.

Talon rose, "I am not an errand boy." He turned to leave.

The immense cat hissed at Talon's rudeness.

"Be polite, Mamet, the boy may leave anytime he wishes." The old man looked up at Talon, "This is not just an errand. It is a...a mission, or you can think of it that way if you wish." He took a labored breath. "I am growing old, too old some would say. The package I need you to retrieve is an item of great importance. I can't go myself, so I need to have someone go in my stead." He leaned over and poked the bread.

"Why me? There are plenty who would gladly take the job."

The old man laughed, "Do you have somewhere else to be? A better job waiting for you?"

Talon remembered his own bleak thoughts. He considered the old man's offer; it seemed an easy enough task, one with little risk. But there was his pride to think of, this wasn't a job for a soldier coming from a victorious war. This was something a servant would do. On the other hand, he *didn't* have any plans. At least it was something to consider. He moved to the fire and leaned against the mantle. "I'm listening."

The old man nodded. He stood and went to the workbench when he noticed the green slime had stopped bubbling. He poured it into a glass bottle and put a stopper in it. After consulting a large book, the old man picked leaves from the various herb pots shelved above the bench and dropped them into a mortar. With quick practiced movements they were crushed and poured into a small satin bag. Talon watched with interest as cobwebs were collected, socks folded, notes scribbled and ashes swept from the hearth. The old man didn't seem to care that Talon was waiting.

When the smell of the bread indicated it was finished baking the old man pulled it from the hearth and took it to the table. He refilled Talon's cup and sat down. Talon joined him. "My name is Olwin of Carthis; I am...an eccentric old man who lives alone, as you see. My health and certain...obligations require that I not leave here. I need someone I can trust to bring me a special pair of rings that are being held for me by a friend. That someone is you." He drank from his mug. "You are younger than I thought, but this may work well in my favor. Few would suspect you of being anything more than an errand boy and that would work in *your* favor."

Talon nodded. "I may be young, but I've got enough experience for twice my age." The tone in his voice told Olwin that this wasn't a boast.

"Then I'll try not to treat you like a young cub." Olwin took a large knife and cut into the warm bread. Buttering it, he handed the slice to Talon. "Are you interested?" He looked into Talon's eyes, ready to catch any hint of doubt in them.

Talon nodded, fascinated by the undercurrent of intrigue.

"You will leave today, taking only the supplies I give you. Travel on foot to Precanlin, and retrieve the package from Marcus, the Rug Maker, and return before the next full moon." Olwin paused and Talon nodded. "I will pay you 20 gold-crowns." Talon showed no hint of surprise at the amount mentioned. "Do you accept?"

Talon took his time answering. There was nothing unacceptable with the task, but it was not his habit to rush into things. Being on foot would fit in with the role of being a simple errand boy, even if it took longer. He would feel naked without his sword, but then he had other abilities to rely on. The money would come in handy. Talon cut another piece of bread, buttered it generously, and took his time eating it in silence.

Olwin seemed unconcerned about the delay to the point of leaving the table to feed chunks of bread to his cats.

Talon finished his bread. "I find your proposition intriguing. I accept the job."

Olwin nodded approvingly and went to a large trunk that stood by itself in a corner. A sweep of his hand displaced a napping cat. He mumbled to himself as he rummaged around. Bits and pieces were tossed out. After some minutes there was a pleased "ah-ha", and the old man rose from his scavenging, holding a long narrow pouch. He picked up a well-worn pack and slipped the pouch into it, and then began stuffing the pack with the flotsam that lay on the floor around him. He returned to the table and passed the pack to Talon. He then went to a cluttered workbench and took a knife from under a pile of books. He mumbled something then returned and handed the knife to Talon. "Everything you will need is in here. You may take whatever food you find necessary from my stores. If you leave right away you should be able to make ten miles before nightfall. I advise you to tell no one about your mission, I have a few enemies that would enjoy detaining you." The old man turned away and busied himself at his workbench.

Talon felt he had been dismissed. He gathered a few loaves of bread, vegetables, cheese and a jug of cider, slung the pack onto his back and left.

Outside the cave he took his horse and walked back toward town. Talon paid off the innkeeper and arranged to have his horse stabled near-by. Judging by the sun, he did indeed have enough light to make it ten miles before nightfall. Talon walked out of town.

## Chapter 2

Shifting the pack higher onto his back, Talon breathed in the pine scented breeze. With a grunt of resolve, he started down the road. It took no time at all for his feet to return to their soldier's quick step. Those feet carried Talon far before nightfall.

Camp was luxurious compared to what he was used to during battle. Talon had found a soft bedroll in the shabby pack. A curious and careless rabbit was cooking nicely above the fire. The bread was soft and the vegetables crisp. There was an abundance of autumn leaves that would make him a comfortable bed and the clear sky assured him of a dry night's sleep.

In the firelight Talon emptied out the pack to see what else Olwin had included. There was an assortment of clothes, some peculiar pouches of herbal mixtures, packets of dried shredded meat, and the long narrow pouch. The contents of the pouch were stiff but light. Opening it, Talon discovered that it contained a flute.

A flute?! What in the world was he going to do with a flute? Shaking his head, he slid it back into the pouch and dropped it into the pack. A light breeze brought the smell of toasted rabbit to Talon's nose and banished all thought of the peculiar old man.

An hour later Talon lay on a comfortable bedroll with a full stomach. Under a perfect sky he closed his eyes and fell into contented sleep.

The next day there were few people on the road. Talon occupied his time by planning little battles in his head. It was a very calm, uneventful day, Talon enjoyed it thoroughly. It was dark before he decided to find a place to camp for the night. He built a small fire and ate a dinner of leftover rabbit and the remnants of his loaf of bread. Talon wearily unrolled his blanket and lay down under a pine tree.

The morning did not hold the contentment of the day before. Wet drops fell onto Talon's face before dawn. He sat up and was greeted with a slap from a damp, drooping limb. His camp was now a large puddle of mud and everything was wet. With a groan he thrust himself onto his feet and surveyed the damage. Wringing out damp blankets and stuffing them inside his pack, Talon broke camp.

Dodging mud holes slowed his walking speed more than he liked. He met up with travelers as he neared a small village. He only stopped long enough to pick up some dry bread. By midday the sun began to dry up the last of the mud. Talon thought himself lucky that there had been few carts to rut up the road.

By the time evening began to fall, Talon was tired and chose the first clearing he found for camp. He took time to build a lean-to but did not hunt for fresh meat. His small smoky fire was short-lived and his meal of bread and dried meat and carrots sat heavily in his stomach as he lay down on the rocky bedroll. It was nights like this that made him long for home.

The next few days of travel seemed to fall somewhere between those first two days. Talon fell into a comfortable routine; he studied the surroundings and people he passed and got through each day with as little effort as possible.

Each night, as he dug into his pack, Talon came across the pouch that held the flute. An odd sense of invitation would flit across his mind, but he hadn't taken it out since that first night. Tonight that feeling of invitation was too strong to be denied. Without thinking, Talon drew out the pouch. He was a bit irritated to find the flute in his hands, but he was in a good mood, this had been one of the better days, and he had a full stomach and a clear sky, so he didn't toss the instrument back into the pack.

He looked the flute over. There was nothing special about it, just a thick hollowed reed with a few odd carvings near one end. With a self-conscious look around, Talon lifted it to his lips. The notes were clear and clean, which was unusual since Talon had never played such an instrument before. His fingers seemed to have a life of their own as they flitted over the holes. Talon was stunned at the music he made. The surprise made him stop playing, stare down at the instrument, and warily put it back in its pouch. He slept fitfully that night and was restless the next morning.

After a dull day on the dusty road Talon was glad to set up camp. Dry wood and a slow squirrel added to his comfort. With a full stomach Talon reached into his pack and pulled out the flute. Odd that he had enjoyed playing the thing. The thought of becoming a troubadour leaped into his mind. The picture of purple and yellow tights, bells on his ankles, a satin jerkin, and floppy hat made Talon laugh the thought away.

The embers within the ring of stones glowed dimly. Talon leaned against a boulder, idly stroking the flute in his hands and staring into the glow. It was late, but he didn't feel tired. In his semi-trance state music seemed to be swimming in his mind. Talon raised the flute to his lips and began to play. No thoughts came between the music in his head and the flute; the notes seemed to have a will of their own. Music flowed around him, as if brought to life, dancing, swaying, rising high and sinking low, spinning wildly, forming the formless. Talon was drawn into it. He felt as if he were drifting free, dancing with the music, flowing with the emotions they brought out.

A shifting ember broke the spell. Talon let his hands fall to his lap, the flute with them. After a few moments he lifted the flute to his lips and began to play again. The magical quality wasn't there, but it didn't sound unpleasant, either. Talon played random notes then began to string them together like pearls. He was amazed at his newfound ability. He paused to take a drink.

A sudden but brief wind brought the embers to life, and Talon warmed his hands.

"Do play some more," requested a deep voice from the shadows.

Talon jumped to his feet and looked around, his hand grasping for a sword that wasn't there. "Come forward and show yourself!" He looked around for some kind of weapon.

"I would rather not. My appearance always seems to frighten people. I find that shadows are so much safer."

The voice seemed large, and over dramatic, but not threatening. Talon was almost ready to welcome the stranger, but movement in the bushes on the other side of the camp made him wary. "There are more of you than you would have me think. Come into the light."

A deep chuckle answered back, "More of me... that's a good one, I'll have to remember to use that some time." A more serious tone took over, "If you insist in my coming into the light, I strongly suggest that you sit down, I would hate to have you stumbling over a rock while running away."

There were suddenly sounds all around Talon. The bushes rustled, something heavy scraped the ground. Shadowy movements began to surround the fire pit. Talon again reached for his missing sword.

When the first huge claw entered the firelight Talon stumbled back against the boulder he had previously been leaning against and dropped to the ground.

"Impressive, aren't they?" The large foot was raised and turned about in the flickering light. The long, spine-covered tail curled around Talon's rock. "Your camp's a bit cramped, if you don't mind my saying so."

"Wasn't expecting guests," Talon mumbled.

Horrible minutes passed as Talon watched the rest of the beast emerge around the fire. Greenish-brown scales as large as his head were layered across enormous thighs, spines sharper than a sword rippled along the back and tail, unthinkable claws retracted as the feet pressed into the ground.

“I have found,” said the deep booming voice, “that most humans prefer to focus on one part of me, rather than the whole, less intimidating. Most tend to fixate on my jaws, though in my opinion, my eyes are my best features.” Talon unconsciously looked into the large, blue eyes, then down at the hugely grinning, fang-filled mouth. “Don’t worry, I just ate.”

The knowledge that he was looking into the face of death made Talon more comfortable, he had faced death in the past, and was not afraid. He began to relax. “Good, I don’t happen to have a cow available for you.” The beast chuckled; at least Talon hoped that was a chuckle.

“My name is Graldiss. I heard your music and thought I’d drop in. It was beautiful. I didn’t think humans had that much depth in them.” One large eye focused on Talon. “But then, I can see that you are not an ordinary human. A bit of the Magic in you, I’d say.”

“Name’s Talon.” He leaned back against his rock and fingered the flute. “Nothing special about me.”

“Don’t be so modest, just being able to keep your wits while surrounded by a Dragon is special in itself. And I can always tell when the Magic is present in a human: a kind of glowing about the head, rather like the glow of the embers in your fire. I ate someone with the Magic once, had gas for months.”

“I feel safer already.”

"Mmm, yes. Well no need to worry, plenty of food around. New villages are popping up all the time." He settled his head on his forelegs. "How about some more of that music?"

Talon couldn't think of a reason not to oblige his guest. He put the flute to his lips, playing a soft tentative note, then another. Graldiss began to hum, many notes lower. Talon closed his eyes and let the music flow out. The deep rumble from the dragon underscored the gentle tune, giving it a haunting quality. They seemed to play for hours.

With a final note, Talon laid down the flute. Graldiss puffed on the fire to re-ignite the embers, then sighed with satisfaction. "Yes, the Magic is definitely there. I haven't heard music like that for ages."

Talon took a drink of water. "I think it's the flute, because I've never played one before. The old man who gave it to me must have put a spell on it."

"That may be a possibility," Graldiss stretched sleepily around the fire, "what is his name?"

"Olwin of Carthis."

"Olwin!?" Graldiss leapt to his feet, knocking Talon over with his tail.

Talon brushed the dirt from his hair and clothes. "Yes, do you know him?"

The dragon looked around nervously. "He isn't here is he?"

"No, he's not." Talon picked up his flute and returned it to its pouch. "I'm just running an errand for him. Got to pick up some rings for him in---"

"Rings!?" A giant foot stumbled through the fire, throwing soot and embers into the air.

"Hey, stop that, or I'm going to move to the next meadow." Talon brushed away the sparks and shook out the blanket.

Graldiss turned his face to Talon, "What does that old wizard want with the Rings?! They should never again see the light of day. Maybe I should toast you after all."

"Hey, calm down. I don't know what you're talking about. I'm just fetching a package, that's all. Don't get all hot about it."

"This isn't just *any* package you've been sent for. If I'm right, you are retrieving the Rings of Ko-Mon Po. They are magical Rings of great power. Olwin's predecessor recovered them and hid them from the world. If they should fall into the wrong hands..." Huge eyes glared down menacingly.

"Wait a minute," Talon became defensive, "I'm not involved in any of this magic stuff, I was hired to do a job, nothing else."

Graldiss withdrew his head. "You didn't know that Olwin is a wizard? Nor the meaning of your errand?"

"He just seemed like an odd old man. Never encountered a wizard before." He paused, recalling his experience in the cave. "Now that you bring it up, I guess you might be right, he did seem to do some strange things." He pulled the blanket over his chest and plumped-up his pack. "I'm just retrieving a package, that's all. Then I'll be on my way."

Graldiss settled his head onto his front legs. "We'll just have to see about that," he mumbled.

"Good night, beast."

"Sweet dreams, human."

Talon's dreams were not very sweet. They were filled with dragons and wizards, battles and shadows.

When the sky began to lighten, Talon stretched, yawned and sat up. He looked around for his gigantic companion, but the camp was empty.

"Must have been a bad dream." He stuffed a couple of dry biscuits into his pocket, folded his blanket, and made his way back to the road.

He was enjoying the quiet walk when he had the distinct feeling that someone was following him. He continued walking, but listened carefully. The sounds of his stalker were not well concealed, leaves rustling without a breeze, the shifting of a leather saddle, and the breathing of a horse. Talon remained calm, aimlessly heading to the side of the road, and behind a tree. He pulled out his knife and waited. When he heard a crunch on the ground he jumped out to catch his 'shadow'.

Graldiss was so startled that he leapt straight into the air, twisting around so quickly that his head got smacked by his tail and knocked himself senseless, plummeting to the ground. The dust raised made Talon cough, and, since he was laughing uncontrollably, this made him as much of a spectacle as the Dragon.

It was some time before they got control of themselves.

"You could get yourself killed jumping out like that." Graldiss shook out a kink in his tail.

"Yeah, and it's not healthy sneaking up on a soldier, either." Talon brushed the dust off of his shirt and picked up his pack. "You weren't around this morning. I thought you might have been a nightmare."

"Why do I seem to always have that impression on people?" Graldiss rubbed his sore nose. "After our talk last night I thought I'd better go and find out what to do with you."

Talon picked up his pack and headed back to the road. "Do with me? What does that mean?"

Graldiss followed behind Talon. "You know, whether I should kill you now or wait until you recover the Rings."

Talon tried to act nonchalant, "Oh, later would be better, I'm sure. Don't want to be too hasty." His mind raced through his options.

"That's what the Matriarch suggested. Seems you've been brought to her attention before. The Matriarch wants me to keep an eye on you."

Talon stopped and turned to face Graldiss. "So you're just going to tag along, until your 'Matriarch' decides I'm enough of a threat and you kill me?"

"Rather unpleasant when you put it that way."

"Is there any other way to put it?" Talon asked defiantly.

Graldiss tried to explain. "You must understand those Rings were the tools used to decimate my race. If there is a chance they will once again come under the control of those who would eliminate us, we must use every means to stop it. Even if that means sacrificing you, I'm sorry if that sounds cruel."

It worried Talon that he understood perfectly. "I could make it easy on both of us and not retrieve the Rings at all."

"No, the Matriarch was definite about not interfering in your errand. Look, if I promise to reserve judgment, would you allow me to join your mission? You're quite interesting, for a human, and I would like to get to know your kind better."

Talon considered for a moment and decided it would be in his best interests to keep this possible enemy close at hand. "I can't very well stop you from following me around, but don't expect me to feed you."

"No problem there, plenty of villages around."

Talon turned to look at his new companion. "You shouldn't be eating people, you know."

"Why not?" Graldiss asked innocently. "They're quite tasty and don't have all that fur. City humans are more plump than those out here on farms, but not as meaty."

"You just shouldn't, that's all. There's plenty of other food around. Besides, people tend to get angry when a dragon swoops down and snatches up a light snack that was their brother. You might find people hunting *you*."

Graldiss had to accept the logic of this. He remembered the stories the Matriarch had told about the Great Massacre. "Well, yes, I see your point. But they're so easy to chew, no horns or feathers, and they don't claw my nose."

"And it gives you a bad reputation. You will find some other food source."

"Fine. As long as I can still burn down a few cottages along the way."

Talon looked into the huge face. "None of that, either. We don't want to be hunted down by angry homeless mobs. Find another hobby."

Graldiss kicked the dirt in frustration.

Talon glanced up and down the road. "Isn't it rather risky being out in the daylight?"

"Dragons don't have many predators, and most humans are too afraid of us to be much of a bother. Wizards, now they're another story. Don't like wizards. Can't mind their own business, always wanting a piece of me. Hard to kill the pesky ones, too. Some aren't too bad, like Olwin, but it pays to stay away from the whole species." The hulking beast began to follow Talon down the road.

Talon thought of something. "Until a few days ago dragons or wizards were just old wives tales. Why haven't I heard about you before?"

"Well, after being slaughtered for centuries, you don't think we'd hang around for you to find us? We've had to hide ourselves. We keep an eye on humanity, but stay out of their way." The dragon shouldered his way past a large oak tree.

"What about wizards? You'd think they'd be running the world by now."

Graldiss chuckled. "Yes, you'd think so. It's not for lack of trying, I'm sure. Normal people are suspicious of wizards and don't give them the chance to seize power. And wizards aren't immortal; a sword can cut through them as easily as any tyrant." He began to hum. "I suppose it's a little early for music?" the dragon asked hopefully.

Talon didn't answer. He started down the road, hoping that his new companion would take the hint and go away. No such luck. It was hard to be unobtrusive with a dragon following behind. Several times the beast would groan and complain when the road narrowed.

"I don't suppose there's an easier way to get where you're going?" Graldiss asked. "These trees are scratching up my nice shiny scales."

Talon turned and glared at the immense figure. "Is there some reason you have to walk along with me?"

Graldiss shrugged his massive shoulders. "Not much else to do today. You seem like an unusual character, I just thought it might be fun."

Talon grunted.

"You aren't very good company, you know. Talking makes the time fly by. Now there's an idea. Why don't we fly? There's not much headwind, and we would get there, wherever *there* may be, much faster than by walking."

Talon looked back at Graldiss. He had to stifle a chuckle at the site of the huge figure spanning the road, trees pressed tightly against his shoulders. "No, I don't want to fly to Precanlin. I would like to be as inconspicuous as possible. I don't think you know how to be inconspicuous. You're a bit clumsy on the ground, aren't you? Why don't you take off, and meet up with me later, if you must."

Graldiss didn't seem put out by Talon's observations and agreed with him. "I'll find you tonight." With a heave of his massive legs he launched himself into the morning sky.

Talon continued on. Now in the quiet he could think about the next day. He was not at all looking forward to entering Precanlin. It had been the one problem in Olwin's proposition. Precanlin was the seat of Baron Taldar's power. Taldar had joined forces with the elder Duke Nidral when it had become advantageous for him. Talon's battle tactics had been instrumental in decimating the Baron's ill trained army. Talon had led the charge against the Baron's son. Now he was heading into enemy territory. Talon spent much of the day's walk planning various strategies that would get him in and out of the city with his body in one piece.

When evening fell, Talon chose an overgrown patch of bushes to make camp. He would not be comfortable, but he wouldn't be discovered easily, either. Though there had been no sign of soldiers on the road, it was better to be careful than captured. Sometime during the night Talon became aware of his large companion curling up next to the bush.

Talon opened his eyes, and shut them quickly against the newly risen sun. The inevitable had come, as the inevitable always does. With a moan, he turned over and would have pulled the blanket over his head if it hadn't caught on a limb. He kicked the blankets off and crawled out of the bushes. It was a few minutes before Talon could stand upright. His joints and muscles were cramped, and he felt has if he had slept under a rock.

"Curious choice for a camp."

Talon searched the still-shadowed bushes for the beast. "I wanted to keep a low profile. Where have you been?" Talon asked conversationally.

"A Dragon's got to eat, you know. I had to make due with a buck. Tricky beasts; got to swoop down on them from behind, if you catch my meaning."

"You're going to get a bit conspicuous as we near Precanlin." Talon crawled out of the bushes.

"Oh don't worry about me; there are ways to keep humans from seeing what they don't want to see." Graldiss stretched and rolled over.

Talon shrugged. He would have liked to have had a warm breakfast, but didn't want to take the risk. Stale bread and leftover rabbit would have to do.

Noises from the near-by road caught Talon's attention. The day was advancing and he'd better join it. He rolled up his blanket, and banished all of his negative thoughts. This is what he had come to do. He would enter an unfriendly city, find Marcus, retrieve the package and get out of the city with all of his body parts intact.

"The road will be busy today, so you won't be able to tag along."

Graldiss nodded his immense head. "Yes, a walking smorgasbord. From the smell of it, there are quite a few soldiers out there," he took a long sniff of the air, "along with a beet farmer, two potters, a weaver, three wagons of ale, a tanner, assorted herdsmen, someone selling perfumes," the dragon winced at that scent, "and various families, mmm, some with small children."

Talon scowled sternly. "Don't even think about it."

Graldiss tried to look innocent. "You know, I could take care of a few of those soldiers for you."

The thought was tempting, but Talon shook his head. "No eating people. It only leads to trouble." He pushed through the bushes and onto the road. "I'll meet up with you later."

The first two miles of travel were spent talking with fellow travelers. Talon was trying to glean as much information about the political climate as he could without seeming too eager for the knowledge. He wasn't encouraged by what he heard. Baron Taldar had grown paranoid and he had allowed the soldiers to remain billeted within the city walls. Bored soldiers made bad neighbors.

His first glimpse of trouble came a mile from the city walls. Ratty-looking soldiers were harassing travelers, making threats, stealing food and jewelry, making unwanted advances to daughters, being downright cruel. This was a bad sign. The Baron was losing control of his army. This worried Talon. The guards at the gate might be a problem as well. They would have the opportunity to take a close look at him, and there was a good chance that they would recognize him. He considered how best to get into the city safely.

Talon stopped and swung the pack from his shoulders. The road was getting crowded, so he could make a transformation without much notice. He pretended to leave the road to relieve himself, and slipped behind a large bush.

Digging through the pack he found a ragged cloak and the flute. He threw on the cloak. With a quick adjustment his neat cap became a floppy hat. He tied some string onto the flute so he might wear it over one shoulder. He looked down at himself to see that nothing would draw unwanted attention, and rejoined the other travelers.

The soldiers on the road made jokes about the scruffy young minstrel, and asked him for a tune, but eventually left him alone for fairer game. At the gates to the city the guards were more concerned with carts and seller's permits to do much more than wave Talon on. So it was the soldiers' laziness more than Talon's ingenuity that got him inside the city walls.

Talon stuck to the edges of the streets, stopping occasionally to glance at a merchant's trays. He kept a close eye on the gangs of soldiers wandering through the market. Near the center of the market Talon spotted the carpet seller's shop. Casually, Talon wandered in.

The place smelled musty, like old yarn that hadn't felt a clean breeze in years. Small colorful rugs hung from ropes strung across the ceiling, larger intricately woven carpets lay in rolled stacks, like logs. The shopkeeper was a thin, sharp-faced man, dressed extravagantly in an ornately embroidered coat. He had a long moustache that dangled past his chin and each side was knotted with a brightly colored string. He did not have the nervous nature of most shopkeepers since his merchandise did not easily slip into the pockets of not-so-innocent shoppers.

The carpet seller spotted Talon and scowled, "What is your business in my shop, boy? You obviously do not need a carpet." The shopkeeper didn't want his shop to become a rest area for over-heated wanderers.

"No, I don't need a carpet. I am here on other business. Are you Marcus?" The weasel-faced man nodded. "I was told by a friend of mine that you were holding a package for him. Some jewelry, I believe."

The dark eyes became wary slits, "And does this friend have a name?"

"Olwin."

The shopkeeper's eyes widened. "The Rings," he whispered. "Come, see how fine the colors are on this selection," Marcus said theatrically. He pulled Talon between a row of hanging rugs. "Has the old wizard died?"

Talon acted interested in the rug's pattern. "A fine piece, indeed." Talon matched Marcus' light tone. "No, at least he was alive when I left him."

"Ah, that is good, yes, very good." He looked around nervously. "And you have come to take possession of The Rings."

"Actually, I am just retrieving them for him."

Marcus grinned and nodded knowingly. "Of course, of course." He led Talon to the back of his tent and thrust a hand into a rolled carpet. When it appeared again it held a dirty bag. From this bag he removed a greasy cloth. Carefully unfolding the greasy fabric, he revealed two gold rings, ornately designed. They were held out to Talon. "The Rings of Ko-Mon Po," Marcus said reverently.

Talon took the Rings. They felt lighter than they looked and they made his palm tingle. Reaching into a pocket, he pulled out a pouch to place the Rings in.

"No, no! The Rings must be *worn!*"

Talon looked suspiciously at the earnest man. "*You* weren't wearing them."

"Ah, but I was just the Keeper. You are the Bearer of The Rings. You must *wear* them."

Talon shrugged and, judging their size, slipped a Ring onto each thumb. The gold felt warm.

The shopkeeper nodded approvingly. "My family's responsibility has been fulfilled," he said solemnly. "Thus have we faithfully executed our role in the conveying of the Rings of Ko-Mon Po unto their rightful possessor." After a reverent pause, Marcus became once again the wily shopkeeper. He ushered Talon toward the entrance of the tent, "I would ask you to take midday meal with me," he said quickly, "but my wife is visiting family, and my cooking can be hard on the unsuspecting stomach. Safe journey." The tent flaps closed quickly.

Talon headed toward the city gates. He stopped for a sweet pie and some apples, glancing at trays of ornaments. He quickly sidestepped a merchant who asked him to play a tune, and was shooed away from a jeweler's tent. His casual behavior drew no attention. He was as invisible as any street urchin.

Within sight of the gates Talon's luck ran out. One member of a party of soldiers, bored with harassing a swineherd, took a long look at the passing minstrel. A quick whisper to a fellow thug holding the swineherd's face sealed Talon's fate.

When Talon realized that he'd been discovered he weighed his options. He was grossly outnumbered; the outcome of a fight would be one-sided. A chase followed by a beating was not appealing, either. There was little to do except to give himself up. He gazed at the sky, the sun, and the dirt. He breathed in the market odors. This would be the last he would see of the world. The blow on his head signaled his end.

## Chapter 3

A hideous laugh was Talon's welcome to the dungeons. A splash of icy water brought him fully awake. Full awareness brought with it the knowledge of being bound hand and foot, and the smell of blood and burning flesh, and of sounds of dying men. Talons' vision focused. The owner of the nasty laugh stood next to him. His face was heavily made-up, bright colors accentuated eyes and lips, exaggerating the eyelashes and brows. His clothes were blue satin, intricately embroidered and sequined. If he weren't carrying a vicious-looking saber, Talon might have mistaken him for a common, if well paid, whore. The fop was Rudrick, Baron Taldar's sadistic son.

"Ah, awake at last. So this is the Great Talon! The boy wonder." he spat. "You know, when I found out that the mighty soldier who had led the battle against us was only 15, I thought it was a joke. I killed the informant myself. But here you are. I'll have to apologize to his family and that's irritating." He smiled at the thought. "I expected so much more from your capture. Not even a black eye or a broken bone. You're no mighty warrior, just a grubby boy. This is not very satisfactory."

Talon didn't comment. He'd heard the rumors and knew the future Rudrick had in mind for him. Talon wasn't going to give him the pleasure of a conversation, and nothing he could say would change his fate.

"A little quiet this morning? Don't worry; we'll have you talking in no time at all." Rudrick personally checked the wrist straps. "Flin couldn't seem to remove those impressive rings of yours." He tapped the band around one thumb. "We'll have to see if a knife will solve the problem."

One of Rudrick's lackeys brought forward a velvet box and opened the lid. Rudrick seemed to examine the contents for a moment, then chose a remarkably ornate knife. The blade itself was excessively serrated. Talon was sure that the sight of it alone had brought forth many confessions.

"I don't sharpen my knives," Rudrick informed Talon, rubbing his finger along the curved ridges, "no sense in hurrying the job. These rings will look nice on me after your blood is cleaned off." Talon's thumb was held down and Rudrick pulled the knife across the flesh.

Talon thought that the wrist straps must have cut off the circulation to his hands, his thumb tingled, but he felt no pain. He heard Rudrick swear under his breath and felt him saw more violently. After a few minutes Rudrick moved to Talon's other hand. That thumb also began to tingle as the blade tore at it. Still there was no pain from the severing of his digit. Rudrick was getting very angry; he swore heavily, grabbed another knife and sawed at Talon's thumb.

The guards mumbled nervously and backed away. Rudrick, obviously shaken, stood back and stared at Talon. He grabbed for a wineglass and downed its contents. "Take him away!"

Guards unstrapped Talon and dragged him to a cell. They threw him in and slammed the door. Talon weakly sat up, cradling his hands against his chest. It took a few numb minutes to come to the realization that his thumbs were still attached, rings and all. There was not so much as a scratch on them. He laughed hysterically. No wonder Rudrick was angry. Talon found a wall to lean against. He didn't question whatever it was that kept his thumbs intact. He could die just as painfully with his thumbs as without. With that unpleasant thought, Talon passed out.

The grating of the lock woke Talon from a very restless night's sleep. Guards dragged him out of the cell, and took him to a bloodstained table and strapped him down. It wasn't long before Rudrick arrived. He looked like he had spent much of the night, and possibly well into the morning, drinking. He grinned an evil grin.

"I've never had someone so young on the rack. Well, as long as you don't count my cousin, that is." Rudrick tightened the straps mercilessly. Standing in front of Talon again, Rudrick rubbed his hands in anticipation. "I prefer to work these devices myself. As you can see, I have the gearing arranged so I can sit comfortable and enjoy the view." He sat in a gaudy, overstuffed chair. A servant handed him a glass of wine. "Now this will hurt immensely, so don't hold back when you feel the need to scream." He began to turn the gear-works.

Talon felt his arms pull tight, and the leather straps tighten against his wrists. He shut his eyes and gritted his teeth in anticipation of the agony to come. The sound of tightening leather began to panic Talon. He prayed that his courage would hold out. He prepared himself for the pain.

The pain never came. The gear turned, the chains pulled, the leather tightened, but there was no pain. Talon felt only an odd tingling from the rings. Waves of tingling flowed up and down his arms. When the chains seemed to tighten to their limit the tingling became so intense that Talon couldn't help but giggle out loud.

Rudrick stood up quickly, overturning his chair. This was not at all the result he was after. Turning in disgust, Rudrick kicked a near-by lackey. "Get this thing fixed at once!" He stormed out of the dungeon.

Talon was pulled off of the rack and returned to his cell. The guards watched him nervously. He made a point of glaring menacingly at a few of them. This time he was not thrown into this cell, but pushed in carefully.

In the dark Talon tried to figure out what had happened. He should have been well on his way to major bodily damage by now, but here he was, totally intact. His only pleasure was in spoiling Rudrick's pleasure.

Some hours later Talon heard the lock grind and the cell door opened. The guard did not come in for him, but ordered Talon out. Talon was led to a table next to a fire pit and his wrists and ankles were manacled to long chains that hung from the ceiling. Talon noticed that the guard's hands were a bit shaky.

When Rudrick entered the dungeon Talon could hear him yelling at some unlucky soul. When he reached the prone body of his victim, Rudrick stopped and composed himself. "I don't know what kind of demon you are, but you will soon be a dead one." With none of his usual pleasure, Rudrick signaled the guards.

Talon was raised off of the table and swung over the hot coals of the fire pit. The heat was immediately unbearable. Rudrick laughed as sweat dripped from Talon's body. He added wood to the already blazing fire. The smell of singed hair filled the air. Once more Talon felt his body tingle, but the heat soon became too much for him and he passed out.

When Talon awoke he knew he must be dead. He lay on a large bed curtained in white, the room was blindingly white, and he, himself, was dressed in white robes. A young woman entered the room and placed a tray bearing something that smelled delicious onto a nearby table and quietly left. The wonderful smell reminded Talon that it had been too long since his last meal. But if he was hungry, then he wasn't dead.

He considered his surroundings and how he might have gotten there. He must still be in Baron Taldar's castle. He got out of the bed and inspected the food-laden tray. He had no fear that the food was poisoned; they could have killed him in the dungeon if they wanted to. But why didn't they? He knew that by all rights he should not be alive. He could think of no logical explanation. Shrugging, he sat down and devoured the meal.

Feeling silly in the long white robes, Talon looked around the room for something more appropriate to wear. He discovered his pack in a closet, but his clothes were nowhere to be found. He tested the door, and was surprised to find it was unlocked. The sound of arguing in the hallway forestalled any thoughts of escape. He moved back into the room and made himself comfortable. The voices halted outside Talon's room.

"...he was responsible for the deaths of hundreds of men!"

"I have heard enough from the guards to know he is something completely different now."

One voice belonged to Rudrick; the other speaker was older and more commanding. It could only be Baron Taldar.

"Those are just rumors, Father, nothing more. I tell you the gears were slipping. There was nothing supernatural about it. And the wood was damp. There was no magic, just incompetence." By the tone of Rudrick's whining it was evident that he knew he was not going to win this battle.

"And the Rings? Were those a rumor too?" Rudrick did not answer. There was a gentle tap on the door and the two entered.

As expected, one of Talon's visitors was Rudrick, not much improved from the day before. The second man was tall and thin. He had a full, long beard, which made up for the lack of hair on his head. The smile on his face was not reflected in his eyes. This was Baron Taldar.

Talon stood, trying to look impressive in the silly robes. "Greetings gentlemen." He knew that the Baron was expecting some kind of special behavior from him, though he wasn't sure what it was. "Would you care to join me for a cup of tea?" he said with a superior air.

Baron Taldar took the offered chair, Rudrick stood by the door angry and suspicious. "I hope your new quarters are pleasing. I deeply regret the terrible misunderstanding between you and my son. He is young and inexperienced."

Talon passed a cup to the Baron. "The error was understandable, if unfortunate. I hold no grudge against you, sir."

The Baron visibly relaxed. "I am glad. If you wish, I will have my son punished for his behavior."

Talon was sorely tempted, but thought it best to not over-play the game. "No need for that, sir. He is just overzealous in his desire for retribution."

"Yes, not the worst of vices, but it tends to get in the way of his judgment."

"My judgment is just fine, thank you. I know a fox when I see one, whatever tricks he has learned." Rudrick stormed from the room.

"I'm surprised you didn't turn him into a toad after what he did to you."

Talon saw the Baron look intently at him, he was fishing for information. "He did very little other than inconvenience me." Talon stood. "If you wouldn't mind, this delay has cost me precious time. I need to be on my way."

Baron Taldar stood and walked to the door. "The events of the past few days have surely fatigued you. I will let you rest." He tapped on the door, a guard opened it. "I'll return later to discuss future arrangements." A cunning smile curled under the bushy mustache.

Talon scowled at the closed and locked door. He didn't like Taldar any more than his son. The Baron had something up his sleeve, and Talon knew it wouldn't be pleasant. He went over the conversation he had heard from the hallway. The Baron considered him more than an ordinary soldier, someone to dress in silk robes and feed handsomely, but also someone to keep under guard. That meant he was valuable. This might work to his advantage. But what did the rings have to do with it?

Talon could not deny something had happened in that dungeon. Something had kept him alive, and had made the guards very nervous around him. Taldar had mentioned the rings. Talon looked closely at them. They were burnished gold, intricately engraved. He gripped one to pull it off but he had no better luck than Rudrick's men. Odd that he hadn't noticed before how tightly they fit. If Baron Taldar thought there was something special about them then Talon could use it to his advantage.

The sun had set before Baron Taldar returned as promised. Rudrick didn't accompany him. "I hope you are well rested. When the weather is better I will show you my gardens, they are quite lovely in the spring."

Talon had not gotten up from his seat when the Baron had entered. "I'm afraid I won't be able to stay here for any length of time, Baron. I have a previous engagement that requires me to be on my way tomorrow."

The Baron smiled and sat at the small table. "As much as I hate to disappoint you, I have to insist that you remain here for the time being." He paid no attention to Talon's angry glare. "You see, since losing so many men in the recent battle, neighboring land owners are beginning to encroach on my land. With your help, I will make them regret their schemes."

"My help? I am not looking for another war to fight, sir."

"Don't be foolish, I don't want a war. I'm thinking of something more ingenious. I'm sure with your...abilities; you can come up with something creative."

Baron Taldar was shrewder than Talon had given him credit for. Talon was still a prisoner, though a bit more comfortably situated than before. "I think you are overestimating my abilities."

"Now now, please don't play innocent. You wear the Rings of Ko-Mon Po; you sit here with me when you should be dead from my son's treatment. If you are not a sorcerer, you are apprenticing to one. Either way, you will come in very handy when I begin my campaign against my neighbors."

Talon knew he was not going to convince Taldar of his lack of magical abilities, so he didn't try. Never one to be considered dull-witted, Talon knew it would be in his best interest to agree to Taldar's scheme and use the time to work out his own plan.

Baron Taldar took Talon's silence as a sign of acceptance, "I will come tomorrow. You can tell me what plans you have for my victory."

Talon was in no mood for sleep that night. He knew Taldar would soon discover he was a fraud and find a way to eliminate him. He checked the door, hoping the Baron had been careless, but he was not so lucky. The windows were tightly grilled. There may be a way to bribe the guard, or the maid who brought him his meals, but that seemed a slim hope.

In an effort to calm himself, Talon took his flute from his pack and began to play. A melancholy tune filled the air.

"Oh, do play something happier."

Startled, Talon dropped the flute. He turned and saw Graldiss looking through the window. He had forgotten all about the dragon. "How did you find me?"

"I recognized the music."

"I am so glad to see you."

"Why, has something gone wrong? You look pretty comfortable there."

Talon looked around. "Yes, but it's a gilded cage. I'm a prisoner."

Graldiss laughed, "How can you be a prisoner with the Rings?"

Talon held out his hands, "Are they really magical?" At least that was confirmed. "I don't know how to work them. They don't come with instructions, you know," he said helplessly.

"Well I guess I'll have to get you out of there." Something distracted him, "Just a minute." He swooped off somewhere. Talon heard a muffled grunt and a guard scream. Graldiss soon reappeared at the window. "They were getting a bit nosey."

"You didn't kill them, did you?"

"No, I just knocked one off of the parapet, the other one ran off. Not very good quality guards, if you ask me. They didn't even *try* to put up a fight."

Talon knew that the guard would return with a whole patrol. "Let's get out of here fast, before reinforcements arrive." He gathered up what was left of his belongings and stood back.

Graldiss drew his tail back then whipped it against the window grate. Plaster and stone chunks flew across the room. Graldiss repeatedly struck the window. The noise drew quite a lot of attention. Guards filled the courtyard, Talon's door opened and a guard stuck his head in and decided that it was time to be someplace else. Within minutes the Baron entered the room. His mouth hung open at the sight of the dragon.

"I'm sorry, Baron, but I won't be able to stay for your little coup," Talon said as he climbed out of the window and onto Graldiss' back, "but I did tell you that I had a prior engagement."

Graldiss beat his wings and they rose into the sky. Arrows from archers in the towers followed them, but they could not match the speed of the dragon. Talon gripped tightly as they rose higher into the air. He felt dizzy from the speed and height and kept his eyes tightly shut.

"You can get off now."

Talon hadn't noticed that Graldiss had landed. He was still numb from the night air. With some effort he uncurled his stiff fingers and slid from the great height. He was grateful for the length of the robe, which kept his legs from being shredded on the way down. He leaned heavily against the dragon's side.

Graldiss set fire to a near-by bush. "Now that's a first, a dragon saving a human. I wonder what they'll say back home." He looked down at his paralyzed companion. "You'll thaw out in a few minutes. Are you hungry? I can go catch us a small bite."

Talon crept closer to the fire. "None for me thanks, Taldar was very gracious."

"He could have given you something better to wear. That robe makes you look silly." He pulled up a near-by tree and set it on the flames. "If you were a prisoner, why did they treat you so well?"

Talon rubbed his hands together. "The Baron had some idea I was a sorcerer. Something about these rings got him all worked up. He was planning to use me to gain control of the surrounding estates."

Graldiss brought his head around quickly. "May I see the Rings?" Talon held up his hands, the gold bands gleamed as brightly as ever. "Has anything unusual happened to you yet?" Talon's silence was answer enough. "I see. Good or bad?"

"I think they kept me alive, so I suppose that would be considered good." Talon looked closely at the gold bands. "What can you tell me about them?"

Graldiss shifted his weight, looking deeply into the fire. After a long silent moment he began to speak, his tone was gentle and rhythmical. "Back at the dawn of humankind, dragons watched your species. We took pity on the small weak human creatures. We collected them together into groups, showed them how to herd animals, how to find and cultivate plants. Later we taught them how to work with metals, build with stone, and harness water.

Soon mankind began to flourish. As cities grew, men became less dependent on us; they had learned how to survive on their own. We knew the time was near to leave them to their own devices. Before we left their leaders were taught something that to dragons was a common everyday practice. Magic." Graldiss' voice turned bitter.

"In our vanity we had foolishly given a mighty power to a race we thought was mature enough to use it for good. Instead, they would only misuse it. We realized too late the mistake we had made. Greed filled the hearts of the leaders, they used their power to increase their wealth and oppress those unskilled in Magic. Wars inevitably broke out and thousands were slain. We tried to correct our mistake by killing those whom we had taught. But humans are quick learners and their power over Magic had grown tremendously. Our lack of subtlety also was a misjudgment. Humans turned against us, we were now the enemy. They destroyed our homes, and killed our young. We were forced to go into hiding.

"One resourceful wizard, by the name of Ko-Mon Po," Graldiss spat, "forged the rings you wear. They protect the wearer from harm, mundane and Magic alike. Po gave the rings to a mighty knight, whose quest was to hunt down the last of our kind and destroy them. They were passed down from generation to generation. A succession of knights brought our kind to the brink of extinction. Our only hope was to find a wizard who believed in the old order, who could be trusted with the Rings and our lives. We found such a wizard in Millius Ragnor.

"Ragnor used his Magic to trick the knight into removing the Rings, and hid them. For centuries the rings were kept hidden from those who would corrupt the world with their powers, and make war upon Dragonkind. Now the rings have been passed on to you. They will shield you from harm."

Talon sat quietly considering everything Graldiss had said, the importance of it weighing on him. The Rings felt hot against his skin, their power making itself known. Talon felt like pulling them off and throwing them away but he knew it would be useless to try. "I can see why you don't like wizards. It must have been a nasty time for you."

A tear formed in the dragon's eye. "My ancestral grandmother sacrificed herself to defend her lair." He shook his head, dispelling the thought. "Now you have the Rings. I wonder if Olwin plans to take you as his apprentice. If he sent you to retrieve the Rings he must think you have potential."

Talon laughed, "Me? A wizard? I don't think so. I'm just a soldier doing a job."

"Not while you have the Rings on, you're not. I can feel the Magic flowing from them."

Talon pulled at the warm gold bands. They did not budge. "You don't understand, I don't want these things, I'm bringing them back for Olwin." Panic began to rise from deep in the pit of his stomach.

Graldiss looked into Talon's eyes, "The Rings would come off easily if you were not meant to wear them. They're meant for you, so you'd better accept it. With those Rings you have the ability to use Magic. You cannot ignore it. That ability must be harnessed and used, for good or for evil. You will have to make that choice." He stretched out and puffed the fire into a blaze and stared into it. "But for now let's get some sleep."

Talon secretly vowed he would find some way to remove those rings; he had no intention of becoming a wizard. As the coals dimmed he relaxed and fell asleep.

## Chapter 4

The next morning Talon's mood matched the weather, cold and damp. Talon was surprised to see Graldiss still dozing by the fire. With a nudge of the foot, the dragon roused himself. The yawn and stretch of a dragon was really something to behold. Talon was sure he saw near-by trees bend and small whirlwinds of dust form. He had to cover his ears at the sound of creaking bone and scale rubbing on scale.

"Mmm, I'm ravenous!"

Talon pulled out a bag of moist cakes he had saved from Baron Taldar's hospitality. "Don't look at *me.* It's every man, or beast, for himself. I certainly don't have enough for your appetite."

Graldiss sniffed the air. "Excuse me, I smell mutton." In the blink of the eye the dragon was gone.

Talon shook his head. "Dragons sure are erratic creatures."

Despite the embarrassing robe, Talon was on the road before dawn and making good time. He wanted to get this job over with as soon as he could, so the faster he moved the better. He would have a lot to think about over the next few days, a lot of unanswered questions.

"What would you like to know?"

Talon stopped and looked around and then up. There above him drifted Graldiss. "Stop sneaking up on me!"

"Sorry, I'll make more noise next time. You want some answers?" Graldiss swooped down and landed a few feet in front of Talon. "You can take that puzzled look off your face. Yes, I can hear what you are thinking. You think quite loudly."

Talon shrugged, would anything surprise him now? "Since you know so much about it...what *is* magic?" He moved to the edge of the road to make room for the dragon's bulk.

Graldiss took up step with Talon. He was silent for a while, trying to fit the definition into words a human could understand. "Magic, is a force of Nature, like rain or sunlight, it is all around us. As a river may be re-directed, a tree fertilized, and the sun and rain obstructed, Magic can be focused, shaped, directed, used as a tool."

"Can I use it to change things?"

"You can affect the world around you, but you can't create rain, or sunlight, you can't cause a tree to grow, or tell the rivers to stop flowing, even with Magic. Do not try to use one aspect of Nature to change another; you will not like the consequences. Accept and use the Magic, and leave the rest to Nature."

Talon thought this through. "You mean I can't pull a flower out of the air, or make the sun turn blue?"

"Partially right. The sun will never change. But, if you know where to find a flower, simply relocate it to your hand, an elementary trick." Suddenly half of the flowers in the nearby meadow rained down on Talon.

Talon stepped out of the fragrant heap and shook the flowers from his hair. "You could have warned me."

"Now you try."

Talon was surprised by the suggestion. "Now?!"

"Yes, why not? No one is looking. Come on, you aren't scared are you?" Graldiss taunted.

Talon *was* scared. He was afraid if he could actually use the magic from the Rings, he would have to accept their power. He was equally afraid, that somehow, this was all a mistake and he would make a fool of himself.

Graldiss felt Talon's apprehension. "It's just you and me, if you make a mistake there's no one here to notice. It's simple, there's a whole meadow of flowers across that fence. Trust the Rings."

Talon was bolstered by his friend's encouragement. "Ok, the idea I can comprehend, it's the method I am uncertain about. Are there magic words I need to say? How about a magic wand?"

Graldiss laughed. "Humans! Always trying to complicate things. Words and objects may enhance the Magic, the *power* is within the Rings you wear, direct their power. Using the Magic is like walking, or speaking, if you spend too much time thinking about how it's done you will lose yourself in the mechanics of it. Just do it, don't think."

Talon faced the meadow of flowers. A picture of what he wanted appeared in his mind. He heard Graldiss sputtering and turned to look. The noble dragon was spitting out a mouthful of daisies. Talon was surprised at the accuracy and the ease of it.

"Fine!" Graldiss picked a flower from between his teeth. "You've passed the first lesson. You can use the art of relocation to make objects *appear* as if you made them out of thin air. But never try to *create* anything. Nature doesn't like having her job usurped." He shook out his wings. "Walking is a bit cumbersome." He rose into the air, gliding in the air above Talon. "Don't make yourself too conspicuous playing with your new-found talent."

Talon started walking down the road again. He thought about everything Graldiss had said. He practiced moving things around and it was much easier than he imagined. He munched on some apples he brought from a nearby tree, and took some clothes off of a line from a near-by cottage.

A thought occurred to him. "Why can you read my thoughts, but I can't read yours?" Talon asked the dragon gliding overhead.

"Human thoughts are quite loud, dragons a bit more subtle. You should take a lesson from the trees -- they know how to quiet their thoughts."

"Trees? Think? You're joking."

"Not at all, a tree's thoughts are the most beautiful; they spend years on a single thought. It's quite an event when they complete one. Now flowers, that's another story. They babble faster than bees, one thought after another, tripping over themselves to come out first. It's not easy to hear another being's thoughts if you can't quiet your own." Graldiss swooped down on an unsuspecting rabbit. He tossed it up, flamed it and swallowed it whole. "Now that you've accepted the reality of Magic, you'll find it easier to do other things with it."

Talon began to consider other sides of magic. If he were able to make things come to him, would it be possible for him to move *himself*? He stopped and looked at a wooded area just off of the road. The thought formed and Talon slammed into a tree.

Graldiss laughed hysterically. When Talon caught his breath, he returned to the road, walking a bit slower. "You have to account for the speed of a moving object, if you throw a rock it doesn't just stop in mid-flight if you tell it to."

Talon decided to delay his experimentation until he knew more about what he was doing.

As the sun began to lower Graldiss flew off somewhere. Talon looked for a secluded spot to spend the night. When he found one he used his new talent to gather wood for a fire. By the time he had laid out his blanket a pile of tree limbs large enough for a bonfire was neatly arranged, and Talon was exhausted. A downward gust of wind let him know that his companion had returned.

"Been busy, I see." Graldiss dropped part of an animal carcass next to the pile of wood. "What are you waiting for? Light it." Talon looked puzzled. "Using magic to start a fire is simple. Heating the wood enough to set it ablaze is the key. Too hot and the wood will be incinerated, not hot enough and you'll have a cold night. Rub your hands together, feel the heat they create. Now transfer that heat to the wood and intensify it." Talon leaped back as the pile of wood exploded into flames. "Now ease back the temperature and let the wood control the rest. Better." He brought his tail around to get warm. "You learn quickly."

Talon cut off a chunk of meat and placed it over his fire, and made himself comfortable. "I see some of the benefits of magic, what are the dangers?"

"If you are careful, you will live a long life. You're a smart boy; just don't try anything stupid, like moving a mountain, or stopping time. You've already seen that using magic can tire you out. You have other options to relocate things. Sometimes *floating* things can be easier. Less effort is needed to push or pull an object. Either way, remember that you need to *see* something to use magic on it. There are some things that are easier to do by hand, like gathering wood."

"I was just practicing," Talon said sheepishly.

"You will need a lot of training. Those Rings can't do everything, you know. If Olwin plans to make you his apprentice, you will have a long road ahead of you. Until you are established as a wizard, be cautious, when things appear and disappear it makes people very nervous. They start pointing fingers and blaming you for every ill that has befallen them. They start boiling oil or heating you over coals. Or they'll use you to make their lives better, with potions and spells. You could become a slave to their whims." Graldiss puffed at the fire. "If you are worried that you may do yourself bodily harm, you're wise to be concerned. If you aren't careful you may transport yourself inside a rock, or find a chair sticking out of your leg. Transporting sticks and flowers takes only little work, but you must take into consideration the weight of an object before you mentally pick it up. Shifting the course of a river or the wind can be overwhelming. Moving yourself over long distances is also very taxing. Just keep it simple and make sure you can *see* where you want to land."

Talon turned the meat over. "What about changing shape? Will the Rings let me do that?"

Graldiss looked over at Talon. "Why? Don't you like the shape you have? No, you are what you are. It is an old fool's tale that a wizard can take on the shape of an animal or a tree. Rather silly if you think about it. It's been tried, of course, but they were never able to change back. If you become an animal you lose your sense of humanness in the process. You may be able to alter your appearance, but you'd better have a good memory if you intend to undo the damage. A better method is to alter the *perception* people have of you. Without changing the way you look, you can project the image of someone else. They see what you want them to see. But remember if someone is *really* looking, they will see through your ruse and a wizard will not be fooled at all. Make the image simple and people won't pay any attention to you at all."

Talon nodded at the wisdom of this. Why make things harder than they need to be. He tore off a piece of meat. "What about you. I don't see you using magic."

"Oh, when I was young I played with magic a lot, moving clouds, relocating cottage roofs, turning friends purple, that sort of thing. But I soon found it tiresome. Relocating boulders above someone's head is only funny for so long." Talon tried to picture Graldiss playing practical jokes, but couldn't quite see it. "When a dragon is full grown there is little need for everyday magic, there's not much a beast my size can't do anytime it wants to. I mainly use magic to keep my appearance hidden."

Talon looked quizzically at his enormous companion, "What do you mean; I can see you very clearly."

"But you know I'm here, others would rather not see a dragon walking along the road, so they don't."

The advantages of such a trick were not lost on Talon. "How is that done?"

Graldiss laughed at Talon's eagerness. "Remember I mentioned making yourself *appear* differently to people?" Talon nodded. "It works the same way, you just match your appearance with that of your surroundings, or blend together the features of people in a crowd and place them over your own." He stretched and laid his head on a foreleg. "It's late; we can talk more about it tomorrow."

Talon "called" for his flute. He played softly, relaxing Graldiss and himself with a gentle tune until he was too sleepy to hold up his head.

A loud boom woke Talon from a deep sleep. Drops of rain brought a groan from his lips. He sat up, scooted under a fallen tree, and pulled the blanket tightly around his shoulders. Though the moon was bright, patches of thunderclouds darkened the sky. In a flash of lightning Talon saw birds flying in the sky below the clouds. With the next lightning bolt he realized that they were not birds, but dragons. The magnificent beasts glided on the air currents as if they were sparrows.

Talon gasped as a bolt of lightning struck one of the dragons. Rather than fall to the ground, the dragon glowed for a moment, laughed and soared higher. As they dove in and out of the clouds, the dragons shouted to each other. In response, the clouds seemed to chase the dragons with lightning. Rather than dodge the powerful bolts, the dragons let them strike and glowing with energy they lit the sky like gigantic fireflies.

One adventurous dragon dove into the darkest cloud. The sky lit up with the brightness of the lightning striking inside the cloud. After a moment the dragon spiraled down. He glowed silver, as bright as the moon. When he hit the ground, sparks shot up. Talon thought the thunder from the cloud sounded vaguely like laughter. The other dragons didn't seem concerned for their fallen companion and continued playing in the storm.

After what seemed hours, the night sky quieted as dragons and clouds tired themselves out. The clouds thinned and separated, allowing the moon to shine through. The fallen dragon rose slowly from the ground, still softly glowing. He joined the others and drifted out of view. A single dragon remained behind.

Talon lay down quickly and pretended to sleep. He knew that he had seen something wonderful and was half afraid Graldiss would resent him for that knowledge.

Graldiss was not in the camp when Talon awoke. In silence he made a simple breakfast of bread and apples. The sun was just beginning to rise when he returned to the road, took his bearings and began walking.

Talon spent the quiet hours thinking about what his life would be like if Olwin took him as an apprentice. Had Olwin known what would happen with the Rings? He would be wise to just hand over the Rings to Olwin and be done with it all. There were easier jobs he could take. He could join up with a band of mercenaries and fight for the highest bidder. There had to be numerous guard positions he could take, he just had to look around. No, he didn't have to become a wizard if he didn't choose to.

This new frame of mind bolstered Talon's desire to get this job over with, and he quickened his step. He didn't get very far. From the knot on his head, Talon thought he must have run into a wall, but there was nothing in front of him. He got to his feet and walked on, but soon found himself on his hands and knees. From ahead he heard a burst of laughter. Graldiss! He held out his hands and stepped slowly forward. It didn't take long to find the rough hide of his humorous friend. He gave a heave. "Get out of my way you silly oaf!"

Like a blurred vision coming into focus, Graldiss appeared before Talon. "Don't you think that was a great way to demonstrate my point about blending in with your environment?" the dragon said, wiping a tear from his eye.

Talon edged past an obstructing claw. "I think it's a bit early for object lessons. If you are going to be giving out instructional tidbits I'd prefer if you do it as we go, I want to get back to Olwin as quickly as I can, and get on with my life."

After a moment Graldiss fell into step with Talon. "You're very serious this morning. You can't mean to tell me you are going to give up the Rings and their power just like that?"

"I don't think I want the baggage that goes along with the power. I've only wanted a simple life. I thought I had one as a soldier, but in war nothing is simple."

"Oh yes, much better to become a pig farmer. I don't understand why you're feeling so sorry for yourself. Magic is a wonderful gift. I think you are being just a bit selfish." With a grunt Graldiss heaved himself into the air.

"I'm fifteen! I'm supposed to be selfish!" Talon shouted.

Traffic on the road became heavier as he neared a fair sized town. Talon felt sure he would be safe entering the town to buy some fresh food. Within sight of the gate the crowd became dense. There were not the usual delays caused by guards checking carts. In fact, there were no guards at all. This was highly unusual.

Once within the gates Talon became more concerned. The crowd was turning into a mob. Something was very wrong. Panic struck him as he heard people murmuring the word "dragon". He forced his way through the mass of bodies. The sight before him chilled Talon.

A cage had been erected in the town square. In that cage, weighed down with massive chains, lay Graldiss. Guards were surrounding the cage, keeping the curious masses back. A hush fell as the local Baron stepped onto a raised platform.

"Good people of Flintcairn, I present the Beast of the Moors!" The crowd cheered. "With great danger to myself I have captured this hideous creature and brought it to you, so that you may witness its destruction!" The crowd cheered again. "The Beast will remain on public display until two days hence when the mighty wizard Keldric will arrive to rid us of this monster!" The crowd went wild, Talon felt sick. The guards stepped back and let the mob close in on the dragon.

In the chaos no one noticed Talon talking to the vicious beast. "Keep your head down," he shouted to Graldiss. The crowd began throwing anything they could find. With Graldiss' head under his forearm, his body was impervious.

"You'd better get out of here," Talon heard Graldiss' words in his mind; "You don't want to be here when Keldric arrives. He has no love for my kind and will make my end a horrible one."

"Isn't there something you can do?" Talon answered back. "You're strong enough to break those chains."

"No. Magic has been used to strengthen them, I cannot escape. You must leave, Keldric will feel the power of the Rings, and if he finds you he will do anything to get those Rings. You must protect them and yourself."

Talon was pushed aside by the angry mob. "No, I won't leave you like this. Let me think of something. I'll return tonight when this madness dies down." Talon ran away from the humility his friend was enduring.

The crowd had indeed diminished by nightfall. Talon waited until late into the night before venturing into the square. He found a sleeping guard and borrowed his coat. In the dark he was easily mistaken for a guard.

"How are you holding up?"

"I'm hungry." Fear laced the dragon's words.

"Have you already tried to get yourself out of here?"

"Yes. It's these chains! They must have been especially made to hold Dragons."

"What about me? Is there anything I can do to break them?" Talon felt helpless, he knew so little about magic, and yet he could think of no other way to help Graldiss escape. "Can't the Rings help?"

"I don't know. If the magic that forged these chains is powerful enough, they might create a paradox. The Rings wouldn't know whether to do your bidding, or protect you from being destroyed by the backlash of magic." Graldiss shook his massive head. "Either way I'd be caught in the middle of the blast and my freedom would be a moot point."

"Isn't there some way I can contact other dragons to help you?" Frustration filled Talon's heart.

"No, they would think it was a trap. They couldn't do anything with these chains, anyway. I think that you should forget about me and get yourself out of here."

"That is not an option." Talon transported a side of beef from a nearby butcher shop into Graldiss' cage. "We still have another day to work this out. Tell me more about the powers these Rings have."

The two talked through the night. By the time the jeering mob again began to congregate Talon had plenty to keep him occupied for the rest of the day. Back at the inn Talon ate a large breakfast and went to his room to sleep. A few hours later Talon began practicing what Graldiss had taught him. He spent the day levitating the bed, making the table invisible, altering the appearance of his room, talking to mice, and making a two-dun piece look like a gold-crown. By early evening Talon was ready to break Graldiss out of his cage.

The streets were busier than usual for a town this size. Having a Monster to gawk at really brought in the crowds. The square filled with the curious and vendors to see to their every need.

Talon found a secluded ledge away from the crowd, but within sight of the cage. He pulled a small gray mouse from his pocket. A quick word and a nibble of cheese and the mouse took off. Within minutes hundreds of mice poured into the square. Just as quickly people poured out; screams filled the air as they ran. There were a few brave souls remaining, so Talon took a bag of his disguised two-dun pieces and dropped them noisily around the corner. The remaining gawkers scrambled to fill their pockets.

Talon stood and braced himself against the wall. With great effort and concentration, Talon cloaked Graldiss in invisibility, and began to raise the cage. If he could just lift the cage high enough, shift it the length of a dragon, and keep Graldiss hidden, the guards might think their dragon had escaped. This would make Talon's *real* task a good bit easier. Sweat ran unnoticed down his brow. His clenched hands had turned white from lack of blood, the Rings were red hot. The higher he lifted the cage, the heavier it seemed. Then, with only a foot left to go, a black wave struck out at him.

Talon was knocked to his knees. When he was able to open his eyes he saw Graldiss visible within the cage, and on the platform next to the cage was an imposing figure in a black robe, an arm was held out before him. The man was turning, searching the crowd. When the ghastly arm pointed at Talon he found himself again in a black void. It lasted no more than a few seconds, but he knew he never wanted to feel it again. He blinked at the daylight when his vision returned. He watched as the robed figure stomped off of the platform and gave instructions to the captain of the guard.

Talon sank back into the shadows. His mind reached out tentatively toward Graldiss.

"Be careful," came the reply.

"What happened?" Talon asked weakly.

"That was Keldric. The Rings were a bit loud, and caught his attention. He blocked their magic from interfering with the spell he'd put on the cage." Graldiss' mind was weak, Talon could feel it fading.

"He looked straight at me, why didn't he find me?" But he knew the answer already. The Rings had made him undetectable to the wizard. They had saved his life, again. "What will happen now?"

"It would be best for us to say good bye. Thank you for trying; you have been a good friend." There was a dreadful silence.

"NO!" Talon's mind rebelled against the bleakness he felt. "Please, Graldiss, hold on just a few more hours, I'll think of something." A resigned sigh filled his mind. Talon returned to his room to recover and think.

Morning arrived too soon for Talon. He had wracked his brain for any possible alternative than to leave Graldiss to die. But it was no use; he had tried everything Graldiss had taught him about the Rings and their power. If Keldric had nullified their magic that avenue of rescue was closed. There seemed to be nothing he could do but to spend the last few hours with his doomed friend. Talon packed his few belongings and went out into crowd.

Keldric had posted extra guards around the cage to prevent another escape attempt. Thankfully the crowds had become bored with this diversion in their lives and there were only a few dozen people milling around the square. Talon took his time, meandering through the stalls, listening to gossip, and locating an unattended side of mutton for

Graldiss. Talon checked on the guards and looked out for the Baron and his wizard. He searched for some last minute rescue.

Eventually Talon joined the small crowd around the cage. When he passed near enough to the guards Talon changed his appearance and blended in with the ring of guards. He moved casually to the dragon's head.

"How are you feeling?" Talon couldn't think of anything else to say.

"I am resigned to my fate. It is an undignified way to end a noble life, but there it is. You should leave before something happens to alert Keldric. He is already suspicious."

Talon's determination to save his friend solidified. "When I leave I'm taking you with me." He looked around at the guards; they were paying more attention to the crowd than to their prisoner. The Baron and his wizard were not in attendance yet. Talon's mind raced through possibilities one more time. The chains could not be broken. The cage was solidly built. The magic involved was too much for the Rings to countermand. If by some miracle he did get the dragon free, Graldiss was too weak to make a safe getaway. A thought occurred to Talon! He pulled an apple from his pocket. Visualizing, concentrating, directing the change. In the blink of the eye the apple was reduced to half its size.

"Yes! Graldiss, I have an idea. But I need a diversion first." With little effort Talon set a nearby hay-wagon ablaze. The crowd's attention shifted. Four of the guards were ordered to help put the fire out; the rest watched the flames with voyeuristic fascination. Quickly Talon turned his attention to Graldiss. Visualizing, concentrating, he placed his hands on the mighty tail for good measure, and willed the change.

The Dragon's startled cry rang in his head. Talon muffled his own cry when the Rings burned his thumbs. The change took only a few seconds, and a few more passed while Graldiss realized what had happened. It was quite a shock to be the size of a house one minute, and the size of a cat the next. Talon pulled his friend out of the oversized manacles and out through the bars of the cage. He stuffed the reduced dragon under his coat and faded into the shadows.

Three streets later, Talon stopped to catch his breath. He pulled Graldiss from under his coat, set him on the ground and looked him over.

"What in the Mother's name have you done to me!?" Graldiss asked in a now tenor voice.

Before Talon could answer the cloaked figure of Keldric appeared in front of him.

"Halt, you pathetic novice! Did you think I wouldn't notice your crude use of The Arts? Who do you think you are dealing with? Your tricks and infantile conjuring are nothing compared to the power I wield!" A bony arm raised, the craggy hand began to glow as a ball of blue flame formed in its palm. "Say goodbye." The arm swung back to throw the glowing ball.

Talon raised his arms to protect himself. His hands became encased in icy agony. He heard a cry of pain and thought it must be his own. Through his half-shut eyes he saw the cloaked figure crumple to the ground.

"The Rings, the Rings!" Keldric's agonized mutterings were muffled in his arms.

Talon didn't wait around; he scooped up Graldiss, staggered through back streets and made his way out of town.

Exhaustion took Talon to the nearest stand of trees. He slid down against a trunk and opened his coat. The condensed dragon fell to the ground.

"What have you done to me?" The sight of the miniature dragon jumping around indignantly was almost comical. "I was a mighty beast, the noblest of creatures! Now look at me! I will be laughed at, ridiculed, shunned! You have made me an outcast."

Talon was too tired to argue. "Better an outcast than a corpse." He piled loose leaves over himself and closed his eyes.

"I'm not so sure about that," mumbled Graldiss before he flew off.

## Chapter 5

A steady rain woke Talon. He wondered if he could use magic to keep himself dry, but decided that would be rather conspicuous, so instead, he wrapped his extra clothing in an oilcloth, and resigned himself to a total soaking. He chose to eat his light breakfast on the road. He had been delayed in Flintcairn far too long. Olwin had said to return by the next New Moon. He would have to quicken his pace to make that deadline.

It wasn't long into the day before Graldiss joined Talon. Thinking himself amusing, the dragon alighted on Talon's shoulder, like a bird, a big, heavy bird. His spirits were definitely higher than the night before. "Greeting, oh thou great and powerful wizard! I see you have chosen to ease your journey by conjuring up this fine sunny day," he said sarcastically.

Talon shifted under the weight of his friend. "At least it reduces the likelihood of running into soldiers along the way. Where did you go last night?"

"I thought I'd better talk to the Matriarch and see what she had to say about this turn of events."

"And what did she say? Will she send someone to eliminate me now that I've abused the power of the Rings?" Talon's tone was light, but he waited nervously for Graldiss to answer.

"You know, she was quite surprised you could manage such a feat. I think she has changed her mind about you." The dragon's tail patted Talon's cheek. "You get to live."

Talon was relived. "What about the other dragons. How did they react?"

Graldiss chuckled, "A few made rude comments but my clutch mates are huge and are quite menacing if they want to be. Anyway, my magic hasn't diminished, so I can pretty well take care of myself."

This made Talon feel better. "I'm glad I didn't *totally* ruin your life."

"No, and I haven't thanked you for saving my life. I owe you a great debt. It was rather a shock, finding oneself reduced as I was, but after a few hours I got used to it, and began to see the advantages of being small enough not to be noticed. I am going to have to rethink my diet, though. No more cattle and sheep, but I was getting a bit fat anyway. Now my menu will include fish, and birds and small fluffy animals of all shapes." The miniature dragon eyed a passing sparrow. Graldiss arranged himself more comfortably on Talon's shoulder. "What adventures do you have for us today?" he said sarcastically.

"No more adventures, please. I just want to get these Rings to Olwin and move on."

Graldiss chuckled. "You make it sound so easy. You might find giving up so much power more difficult than you think."

Talon hadn't considered that. There were definite advantages to magic. This gave him something to think about while he walked.

Night fell, and Talon set up camp under a large oak. Graldiss had provided a plump rabbit that was roasting over the fire. Talon had taken out his flute and began playing, Graldiss sang along. Magic seemed to hang in the air around them. Four potatoes joined the rabbit over the flames, a cherry tart and a tankard of cider appeared next to Talon's feet. When the rabbit was cooked they ate their feast.

"Some poor woman is trying to explain to her husband why his dessert is missing." Graldiss said blandly.

Talon felt the guilty weight of his full stomach, and quickly changed the subject. "Back at Flintcairn, Keldric knew someone was using magic, and he eventually found that someone was me. How, did he do that?"

"I described magic as a force of Nature. You can feel the breeze of the wind, the warmth of the sun, or the growth of a tree (if you are sensitive enough). The same is true with magic; when you use it, others, who are receptive to it, can feel its energy. Your unguarded use alerted Keldric, but the blast that occurred when you shrank me was like a beacon. You will find it's best to limit your use of magic when you are trying to be inconspicuous."

Talon nodded in agreement. The mention of Graldiss' transformation brought up another question. "Is there a way I can return you to your normal size?"

The Dragon shook his head sadly, "The Rings are powerful enough for one transformation, but I'd rather not risk trying to reverse the process. I am just grateful to be alive." He curled up next to Talon and closed his eyes. Talon took this as a sign to call it a night.

The next morning Graldiss was nowhere to be seen. The moon Talon had seen the night before was getting too full for a casual pace. He grabbed a cold breakfast, packed the bedroll and started quickly down the road.

The small dragon showed up before Talon got too far. "Any luck?" Talon asked.

"A few lazy chipmunks." He took his place on Talon's shoulder.

It wasn't long before they were joined on the road by other travelers. Some of them noticed the peculiar lizard on the vagabond's shoulder; others were too busy with their own thoughts to bother with anyone else.

Talon was also wrapped up in his own thoughts and his normally sharp senses were dulled. He did not notice that one of his fellow travelers had drawn next to him and was matching his pace. And another was moving up behind him. Graldiss was sleeping off his breakfast, so he did not see the newcomers either, until too late.

The man at Talon's side stepped quickly in front of him and stopped, and the one behind pushed in close. Talon's wits came awake, he reached at his side for his sword that wasn't there, he cursed. He crouched low and turned sideways to face both opponents.

"I have nothing of value, so go after riper pickings."

One bandit pointed a short-sword at Talon's hands. "Those rings look valuable enough for me. Let's have those off, if you please."

Talon felt the bands on his thumbs begin to warm.

"Be careful," the second bandit warned his partner, "remember what we was told 'bout this guy."

The first bandit nodded and brought the knife close to Talon's throat. "No tricky moves, kid. Just hand over them rings slow and easy and we'll let you go with yer head still attached to yer shoulders." The point of the second robber's sword dug into Talon's side.

Any hope Talon had that the fellow travelers on the road would assist him were short lived, they avoided the unpleasant scene with quick side-glances. Graldiss was now fully awake. He whispered: "If you'd like I can toast this guy." Talon shook his head.

Talon took a step back to give himself room to move. "Please, mister," he said innocently, "don't hurt me. I'm just a kid."

"That's not what we was told." The second bandit said knowingly.

The bandit with the knife lowered it slightly. "Just take off the rings and we'll be on our way."

Talon made as if to pull off one ring, tightened his arm and lunged at the bandit behind him, digging his elbow into unprotected ribs. Then he dropped to the ground and kicked out at the knee of the other. Graldiss clawed at one face while Talon threw dirt in the other. Arms, legs, tail, it was hard to distinguish one body from another. Smoke and clouds of dust obscured the melee from curious on-lookers. Small streams of flame were followed by shouts of pain. After quick mental instructions Graldiss flew off into the trees to hide. Talon rolled free from flailing arms and blended into the watching crowd. Very gently, he masked himself in the appearance of a young farmhand.

It didn't take long for the two thieves to come to the conclusion that their target was no longer in the fight. With anger and chagrin they searched the dispersing crowd.

"That sorcerer ain't going to like this." One said, dusting off his shirt.

"When he finds out we'll be long gone." They made no haste in heading *away* from Flintcairn.

Talon kept his altered appearance for a few miles, just to be safe. Graldiss showed up later that afternoon, when the travelers thinned out and Talon was alone on the road.

"Well that was exciting." The dragon curled around Talon's neck. "Who sent them?"

Talon shifted under the added weight. "I'm pretty sure it was Keldric. I'm beginning to really dislike that man."

"He's not noted for his friendly manner." Graldiss said sarcastically. "You've made a powerful enemy."

Talon tried to shake Graldiss off. "Is there a reason you've decided I'm to be your mode of transportation?"

"Flying isn't as convenient with these tiny wings you've given me, so I'm giving you the honor of carrying one of the most majestic of beasts." He curled his tail under Talon's chin.

"I thought you were getting over that."

Graldiss chuckled and tickled Talon's chin with his tail.

Rain began to drizzle down, Talon moved to walk under the tree-lined edge of the road. In an attempt to lighten his mood, he transported the flute to his hand and began to play a cheerful tune. After a few moments Graldiss joined in, his humming was much higher pitched than before, but beautiful nonetheless. To Talon's surprise, Graldiss began to sing. Talon had never heard his friend's native language before. He almost laughed at the yodeling quality of it, but there was so much heart in the tone and rolling crescendos that he played with more passion than ever. When the song was over the two were silent again. What could they say? It was long after sundown when Talon stopped to make camp. Graldiss lit the fire, pleased to find his flame only slightly diminished.

The remainder of the journey took three blissfully uneventful days. Talon was anxious to get some answers out of Olwin. He found his steps slowing as he entered the meadow where Olwin's cave was hidden. There was no logical reason he should be nervous, he would drop off the rings, pick up his money and that would be that. Talon had convinced himself that once the Rings were gone, the magic would be gone as well and he could get on with his life. He had gotten along just fine without magic. He felt as if he were trying to rationalize his decision. His companion didn't help matters. Talon could feel Graldiss tensing on his shoulder.

"If you grip any harder you'll draw blood. Why are you so nervous?"

Graldiss shifted self-consciously. "Wizards and Dragons have been mortal enemies for centuries, you don't just change that overnight. You saw Keldric; he would have happily vivisected me and parceled my body parts out to the highest bidder." Talon felt his friend shiver. "I'm only here to see this adventure through to the end."

Talon was glad of the company, he felt more than a little apprehensive about being in the company of a wizard. His recent experience with Keldric made him weary.

Talon found the cave entrance easily. The cave passages looked as if they had been cleaned out since the last time he had been there. The piles of debris were neatly stacked, and the floor freshly swept. Glowing torches lit the darker recesses. The blanket had been removed from the entrance to the cavern. Talon called out a hello before entering, but there was no answer.

The living area had also been cleaned up. Shelves were organized and the workbench was clear and newly scrubbed, the pile of ashes in the fire was gone. The cats were gone as well. This scene made Talon a bit nervous. "Olwin!" There was still no answer. "Is anyone here?" he called out.

There was a rustling in an alcove, a sleepy moan. "Is that you, boy?" The curtains were moved aside. The old man lay on the cushioned bed, looking very frail. "I am glad to see you." He tried to sit up, but managed only to move higher onto his cushions. "Don't stand there, come closer."

Talon put his pack on the table and pulled a stool next to the bed. Graldiss flew to the fireplace mantle. The man on the bed before him looked drained of life; thin, and weak. This worried Talon more than he cared to admit.

"Don't look so concerned, I'm not dead," a chuckle cut the tension. Olwin managed to push himself up, swung his legs over the side of the bed and stood up. With a wave of the hand his nightshirt was replaced with a bright yellow tunic and breeches. He swore under his breath and waved his hand again. A more respectable gray robe replaced the outlandish clothing.

Ignoring Talon, Olwin glared around the cave. "Never trust an enchanted cave to leave your stuff alone." With a wave of the hand the workbench became cluttered with bottles and wrinkled pages, assorted cats appeared and climbed onto chairs. "Go to sleep for a few weeks and look what it does!" A fire started in the hearth. "I'm famished. Nothing like an extended nap to increase one's appetite." His eyes widened as he noticed the green dragon above the fireplace. He put out a finger as if to touch, but thought better of it. "Interesting. I didn't think they came in that size." Graldiss snorted. "Doesn't seem very friendly." A platter of meat and bread appeared on the table. "If your friend is hungry I can bring in a rat or two."

"Don't bother," Graldiss hissed, "your cats look plump enough." The dragon swooped close to a sleeping cat, and then swerved to land by the hearth.

"Testy, isn't it?" Olwin commented, slicing meat and cheese.

"Wouldn't you be if someone offered you vermin for lunch?"

Olwin smiled at his faux pas and set about making a sandwich. "I must say that I expected you sooner than this. Were there difficulties?"

Talon ignored the snort from the hearth. "Oh, nothing I couldn't handle," he said flippantly, plopping down into a fireside chair. "A little torture, a bit of magic, nasty wizards and robbers, that's all." Talon went into detail about his adventures while Olwin ate.

Olwin tossed his last bite of bread to an awaiting cat and joined Talon by the fire. "Well, that was more than I expected when I sent you out into the world." He didn't seem at all surprised by anything

Talon told him. Olwin chuckled, "A dragon! Now that thought never even entered my mind. It was the music, of course. I should have thought of that, but I had other intentions when I included the flute. Yes, the flute has magical properties," he answered Talon's accusing stare. "Its music gathers ambient magic to its player. It's often used to strengthen a casting spell. I suppose a nearby dragon could be called ambient magic," he chuckled again.

Graldiss puffed himself up indignantly. "Dragons aren't dogs. We don't come when called by humans."

"Can you think of any other explanation as to why Talon isn't part of some heap of dragon poop, right now?" Graldiss didn't answer. "You were attracted by the music, intrigued, and stuck around. Not the usual actions of a dragon."

Graldiss shrugged and let Olwin think what he wanted.

"I thought the flute's power would begin to bring out your own abilities."

Talon was stiff with anger from the revelation that he had been manipulated. "And the Rings? You knew what they would do to me, didn't you."

"*For* you, to be precise. Yes, of course I knew, I'm old, not stupid." With a wave of his hand, the embers found renewed energy. "But you are giving far too much credit to them. The Rings of Ko-Mon Po were created to protect the wearer from coming to harm through magic, nothing more." Both Talon and Graldiss were taken by surprise by this statement.

Graldiss was the first to speak. "That cannot be! How could so many of my kind have been killed if the Rings had not given immense magical power to those who wore them?"

"I'm sorry to have to be the one to break the news to you, but it's true. The knights that decimated your race had no magical abilities other than the protection from magic. Being creatures of Magic yourselves the Rings protected the knights from all the fire-breathing, claw-slashing, and teeth crunching. They could be hurt just like anyone else. A well-aimed boulder might have saved your species a lot of trouble. The ferocity and tenacity attributed to those brainless knights was all their own. Po actually made those rings not to protect him against dragons, but from his fellow wizards. He wasn't very popular."

An old blanket appeared around Olwin's shoulders. "It was through a particularly clumsy knight that my predecessor eventually gained control of the Rings. A knight named Crendill was attempting to cut off the tail of his latest prey when his sword slipped and he cut off his own hand. The idiot was wearing both Rings on that hand. The quick-witted dragon took advantage of the situation and swallowed the appendage whole. It gave him quite a nasty case of indigestion. Poor thing appeared at my predecessor's door one night doubled up with pain. Ragnor gave the beast something to speed up his digestion and within an hour he had a smelly pile of dragon manure on his front lawn. The dragon was so relieved he forgot all about the Rings. Ragnor found them while cleaning up the smelly mess. Over the decades they've been kept hidden. And after I've taken care of whoever is trying to kill me, they will once again be put into hiding."

"That doesn't explain why I didn't have my limbs torn off in Rudrick's dungeon. I'm sure those were not magical torture devices. "

Olwin looked puzzled for a moment. "I would guess that in your heightened emotional state your innate magic was doing everything in its power to protect you and striking out with such wild fierceness that the Rings were really keeping you from harming *yourself*."

Talon sat silently for a while, trying to understand everything he had just learned. He couldn't voice the fear building inside him.

Graldiss felt no such hindrance, "You mean to tell me Talon's magic had nothing to do with the Rings?! How can that be? He's had no training, no power transference. He's just a soldier!"

Talon waited for the answer, dreading it.

"I don't know for sure how he came to be what he is. I've been reading Wizard History, trying to find record of untamed magic within a human, but found nothing more than old wives tales about pregnant women coming into close contact with a dragon and infusing their unborn children with magic, but nothing was ever proven."

Talon stared into the flames, "You must be mistaken; it has to be the Rings. I am no wizard, I didn't even really believe in magic until this happened."

"There is one way to tell. Give me the Rings."

Talon skeptically took hold of one band and twisted it. The ring, which up to now had held fast to his digit, slid free as if it were too large for the thumb it encircled. The other followed, with similar ease. He stared at them.

Olwin took the Rings from Talon's open hand. "Don't be so surprised. They weren't meant for you, you were only the Bearer of the Rings. They would have come off anytime after you came into the cave." He slid the rings onto his own thumbs. "Now, why don't you try some magic?"

This wasn't going as Talon had planned. He had gotten rid of the Rings and now he just wanted to get away. But he knew he would never be free from this cloud until he proved to himself that any magic abilities he had, left with those Rings. Thought took form and an indignant cat found itself on the cold stone floor instead of the soft cushion that was now in Talon's possession. With a moan Talon threw the pillow across the room. "Why now? I'm just an ordinary person. Did the Rings trigger it?"

"No. The night we met, I knew the potential was already there, just hidden. It was rather startling to walk into the tavern and feel so much power. When I realized you knew nothing about it, I felt I had to do something to bring it to the surface. Eventually another wizard would have discovered your secret and he may not have been as nice as I was to you." Talon looked dubiously at Olwin. "Wizards have been known to kill to gain the powers of another."

"So retrieving the Rings was just a ploy to bring out my hidden talent?" Talon was looking for someone to blame for his troubles.

Olwin leaned down and stoked the fire. "Not at all. I needed the Rings to foil a plot against my life. Finding you just meant I wouldn't have to recover them in person. If you hadn't discovered your talent on your own by the time you returned I would have broken the news to you myself and risked your not believing a word I said. I'm glad it worked out as it did. And I am very glad you had such a competent instructor." Olwin raised his mug to Graldiss in acknowledgment of his part.

"What happens now?" Talon asked grumpily.

"What do you want to happen? And don't say you want it all to return to the way it was, because it can't. I'm sure your friend has told you that already. You can stay here and I can teach you what I know, or I can find someone else to train you. You *do* need training, make no mistake. Inside you, and all wizards, is an immense power. You can use your power for good or bad, that's your choice and your choice alone. But you can't just walk away and ignore what you are, nature won't let you."

Talon stood and walked to the cavern entrance. "I can ignore it for tonight." He turned and walked out.

Graldiss flew out after him. "Where are we going?"

"To town. I need a bath and a good night's sleep."

Talon was surprised to see some of his fellow soldiers still in town. He returned to the inn he had stayed in three weeks earlier. He gathered his belongings from the stablemaster and carried them to his room. After a warm bath and a nap, Talon went down to the tavern to get a bite to eat. Graldiss judiciously chose to remain in the room. He had discovered how comfortable a feather mattress was.

When Talon walked into the tavern he was recognized and hailed by his acquaintances. They inquired after Talon's health, and asked him about future plans. The men chatted on about jobs they had accepted, ladies they had met and reminisced about battles they had won. Talon sat and listened to them all. He wished he could go back in time three weeks and ignore the odd old man that offered him a job.

Talon got little sleep that night. The revelations Olwin had sprung on him and the uncertainty of the future brought out hundreds of questions. Talon didn't always like the answers he came up with. He felt as if his world had been turned inside out and twisted into a knot he couldn't untie.

By first light, Talon had come to terms with the *idea* of being a wizard, but decided it would be on his own terms, whether the old man liked it or not. He packed his few belongings, leaving his battle-scarred armor behind on the bed. He paid the innkeeper, sold his horse and walked out of town. Graldiss joined him on the path to Olwin's cave.

"Doesn't look like a good night's sleep did you any good."

Talon paid no attention to the comment. "I'm surprised you're still around. You found out about the Rings. I thought you would have wanted to get as far away as possible."

The small beast floated lazily above Talon's head. "That had been my plan, but I was told to stay with you."

Talon stopped. "Told? By whom? Not Olwin?"

Graldiss landed on a tree limb. "No, not that old wind bag. The Matriarch paid me a personal visit last night. It seems she knows something about you, and wants me to keep an eye on you, to help train you."

Talon shrugged and continued on his way. "Well, I certainly don't mind, though why a dragon matriarch would bother about me is a total mystery."

Graldiss took his place on Talon's shoulder. "Sometimes it's best not to ask. So, what are your plans?"

Talon strode through the cave entrance. "If I'm going to become a wizard, I'm going to be the best damn wizard there ever was."

Graldiss shook his head, "Well, there's modesty for you."

## Chapter 6

Talon found Olwin thumbing through a tiny book, looking at it through a viewing glass. Three knives were busy cutting vegetables, and the cats were eyeing the roast turning on the fireplace spit. Talon tossed his pack on a chair and buttered a slice of bread. Olwin put down the viewing glass and waved Talon to the bench.

"Have you made your decision?"

"I didn't have many choices." Talon grumbled with his mouth full. "I'll stay, and learn what you have to teach me."

Olwin nodded. "Where's your friend?"

"Graldiss had some errands to run, dragon business, I guess."

"Well let's get started, the roast won't be ready for some time." Vegetables flew across the cave and into a boiling pot. Olwin searched through a stack of dusty books. He pulled one out, opened it, and flipped through the pages. Talon noted the dust didn't move from the book's cover, but stayed as if it were part of the binding. "Ah, here it is, the first lesson."

Talon read the title of the page: "How to Move Enemies and Influence People."

"One of my better spells. Can't keep people far enough away, in my estimation." Olwin went to check the vegetables.

Talon looked through the book. 'How To Change A Bear's Mind', 'Finding The Wrong Mushroom For Any Occasion', 'Getting Your Socks To Smell Like Roses', 'How To Season Eel'. He glared at Olwin. "What *is* this? This doesn't look like a book of magic spells. 'How to Peel Grapes'? This is *not* my idea of Wizard's Magic."

Olwin dragged a stool to the workbench and sat down. "And what, pray tell, do you think a wizard does? Run around changing the weather, fixing people's lives, deciding the fate of the world? When would we find time to sleep? Wizards are, at heart, a lazy group of men, and we use magic to make our lives easier. We use it for everyday things, stirring soup, sweeping the floor, or moving a rain cloud over the garden. Great acts of magic tend to backfire, or lead to a chain of events we can't control." He twirled a green feather in his hand. "And as for helping people, take some advice, stay as far away from them as you can. There are only two types of people: the kind who want to use *you* for your magic, and the kind that want to stone you *because* of your magic. Mankind can take care of itself. What we do will make little difference when the Gods decide the game is over."

"Then what is the use of having the power? Sounds like a waste of talent." Talon knew he could never be so indifferent.

Olwin leaned against the workbench and pulled out a pipe. "There are *some* wizards who meddle in the lives of Normals. A few hunger for power, and use their arts toward that end, but they are the minority. Some wizards think that if they can control enough powerful men, they can mold the world to their idea of perfection. Trouble is, these powerful men aren't very popular, and they tend to get killed on a regular basis. Then there are wizards who live in villages, trying to ease the lives of the residents, but it's like trying to dam up a river with pebbles. Most of those wizards wear themselves out before they hit their first century and spend the next one recovering. Not many isolate themselves as I do. Can't stand the sound of their own voices. I get the occasional supplicant; I figure if they can last five minutes of my bad temper they must really need my help. But I don't let them think they can come around whenever they want to. A crotchety hermit, that's what you should aim for."

Talon decided not to argue with the old man. He flipped back through the pages of the dusty book and read aloud:

"'How to Move Enemies and Influence People.

For highest potency be in eye-shot of the victim.

1) Plant feet apart, firmly on level ground. If possible brace yourself against a tree.
2) Clear your mind of distracting thoughts.
3) If politeness is required, give the victim verbal warning.
4) Visualize the victim's destination, take into account any shrubbery that may be used for the landing (there is a wonderful bramble patch next to Kittery Lake).
5) Draw in energy from your surroundings.
6) Send a "push" to knock the victim off balance.
7) With a mental sweeping movement, relocate the victim.
8) If audience reaction is necessary, add some choice gibberish and gesticulation.'

"This seems straightforward enough. Nothing unusual."

Olwin was insulted. "Well of course it seems simple now, but before I came up with these steps wizards would "pick up" whole chunks of space and mentally carry their victim away. Very wasteful of energy. I streamlined the whole process."

Talon rolled his eyes, but had no chance to comment as Graldiss swooped in and landed on his shoulder. "Did I miss anything important?"

"Speaking of streamlining, this is truly amazing work." Olwin moved to get a close up look at the dragon. "The proportions are perfect." He lifted a wing and flapped it. "There seems to be no loss of stability."

Graldiss pulled his wing out of Olwin's grasp. "Do you mind!? I'm not a sideshow oddity, you know."

"My apologies." Olwin sat back on his stool. "How did you do it?" he asked Talon.

"Actually, I didn't think much about it at the time. Graldiss was about to be killed and I had tried everything else I knew. The idea popped into my head and it just happened. I offered to undo it, but Graldiss declined."

"Very smart of him. Uncontrolled magic takes over when strong emotions are involved. Once the heat of the moment is over and the brain is again in control, such complex magic is nearly impossible. One miscalculation in the enlarging process and ...well let's just say that he's better off with his new size than dead." Olwin stood abruptly. "Well, this isn't getting anything done." He led Talon to a faded curtain. He pulled it aside, revealing a passageway.

"Down this short passage is a small cavern, probably dirty. It's all yours. Lunch will be ready in about 20 minutes. Tomorrow I'll start teaching you everything you'll need to know to survive the next few hundred years." The old man turned his attention to the fire.

With a shrug, Talon picked up his pack and went through the passageway. The tunnel was tall enough to walk comfortably up right, and opened onto a dark cavern. Building up heat, and cautiously releasing it, Talon lit a stack of rubbish. Once there was enough light to see, he relocated the fiery heap to the small fireplace along one wall. Talon *borrowed* some of Olwin's woodpile. In the light .of the fire, Talon looked around his new quarters. The floor of the cavern was heavy with dust, only a few tiny mice paw prints marring its smooth surface. A sleeping shelf took up one wall, a narrow workbench stood next to the small firepit. There was little else in the room.

"What a dump!" Graldiss daintily landed on the workbench.

Talon agreed. He moved around the cave, picking up and tossing trash into the fireplace, setting upright a toppled chair, shaking out a dusty blanket.

"What are you doing?" Graldiss asked. "You're a wizard, stupid, you don't have to clean this place by hand."

Talon laughed, "Hadn't thought of that." In a suffocating puff, all the dust and cobwebs blew up the sooted chimney. He relocated some clean blankets from Olwin's shelves, as well as cups, plates, wood, loaves of bread and water jugs. With a final nudge, he fixed the wobbly chair and went back to the larger cavern.

Olwin was still at the workbench, he was holding his hand over some book, both were glowing. Not wanting to disturb the old man, Talon cut a slab of meat and took it to the table. It wasn't long before Olwin joined him. "More difficult than I thought," he said, more to himself than Talon. "May be using a third party, or a talisman."

"You mentioned someone was trying to kill you." Talon hoped to trigger the storyteller in the old man.

Olwin nodded. "Noticed it last year. Sneaky little buzzard, that's for sure. Started out slow: achy bones, sore muscles, that sort of thing. Well I'm 204 years old, for pity sake, I didn't think anything of it. Then I began sleeping for weeks at a time, forgetting things, not eating. I started looking for physical reasons. It took me a few years to rule out all the normal possibilities, but I had to be certain. When I fell out of a tree last year I knew for sure, someone was trying to kill me."

"Fell out of a tree? Forgetting things? Achy bones? Doesn't sound sinister to me."

"After your first few decades as a wizard you'll find out you aren't like Normals, your foot may slip on a patch of ice, but you'll automatically spell yourself from falling. It's one thing to forget to wash your face for a week or two, but you never forget where you put your mugwort. I *know* someone is trying to get rid of me. I wouldn't have brought the Rings out of hiding unless I was sure. I'll keep their reemergence a secret until I've figured out who's after me."

Talon guiltily looked away. "That might be hard," Talon said slowly. "I think it's safe to say at least one wizard knows they're back." Olwin had the look of a parent waiting for an explanation. "Well...there was this wizard who was trying to kill Graldiss. He attacked me while we were escaping, and happened...to notice...the Rings." Olwin waited for the rest of the story. "He sent some thieves to take them from me. Baron Taldar seemed to know about them, too."

"Did you happen to catch the wizard's name?"

"Graldiss said his name was Keldric."

Olwin swore in some obscure language. "Hundreds of years of careful concealment blown by a careless boy."

Olwin's indignant tone irritated Talon. "You didn't bother to mention that I was supposed to keep these things hidden! If Marcus hadn't insisted that I wear them, the Rings would still be a secret. But you just had to play your games, old man. So don't start blaming me for your troubles."

Olwin made no comment. He went back to his workbench. "If Keldric knows of the Rings, then I may be able to use it against him." He began mumbling to himself, and his train of thought shifted away from Talon.

Talon felt dismissed. He picked up the large dusty spell book and a loaf of bread and went back to his chamber. He found Graldiss curled on the bed.

"I don't know about this wizarding business." Talon dropped the book on the table. "They seem to spend half their time making their lives more comfortable, and the other half making trouble for others."

Graldiss flew to Talon's shoulder and looked at the book. He laughed at the spell Talon had turned to: "Keeping the Home Fires Burning", the instructions were a long and complicated list of steps to keep cottages warm. "I suppose they wouldn't think of something as mundane as putting a log on the fire."

Talon had to agree. "Magic didn't seem as complicated when *I* used it."

"Maybe they feel more important with all this hocusy-pocusy stuff added on. After hundreds of years it's probably part of the training."

"I sure hope not. I'd feel silly waving my arms around and saying: 'Bring heat and light unto this home so that it may warm the spirits of those residing within its walls'," Talon read from the yellowed pages. "I'd be laughed out of town."

"The words don't mean a thing," Olwin stood in the cave's opening, "but sometimes you need to be dramatic to get your point across." He looked around the small cave and nodded his approval. "Nice work. As your friend pointed out, the theatrics are a hold over from centuries of archaic training." An old rug materialized and unrolled in front of the fire. "Well, you've proven that you can use magic to make things happen, but there are dangers in just throwing magic around. Humans aren't the only beings that can use magic. Of course there are the dragons," Olwin nodded toward Graldiss. "In fact, most animals have some innate protection magic. There is also magic in plants, and in the very ground we walk on. Much of what you will find in my books will deal with harnessing ambient magic. Taking from them what you need."

A bag of coins appeared on the table. "If you're going to be staying here, we'd better stock up on food. Snatching for one person is less noticeable than for two. You'd better go down to town and buy some supplies."

When Talon had gone Olwin looked accusingly at Graldiss. "Why don't you tell me what you're doing with that boy?"

Graldiss made no attempt at innocence. "The same thing you are. We're keeping an eye on an unusual boy, and making sure he's trained properly." Graldiss tried to sound indifferent. "We wouldn't want him to fall into the wrong hands."

"Why is Magrid concerned with a young wizard? She has not dabbled in our affairs for centuries."

Graldiss shrugged. "We knew right away the boy was different, he didn't *smell* like a wizard. The Matriarch wanted him watched, I volunteered. She nearly fainted when she heard the boy was to retrieve the Rings of Ko-Mon Po. Did you know that when he put the Rings on they rang out so loudly we could hear them for a hundred miles?"

"So much for subtlety." A thought suddenly occurred to Olwin, "Do the other colonies know about the boy?" You would have killed him before now if that had been your plan and now you aren't large enough to protect him. So you're just going to sit around and watch me train him?"

Graldiss paid no attention to the jibe. "I am just supposed to watch him. When we saw that he could use the power of the Rings it became a very dangerous time for him. If he'd shown the least tendency toward evil I would have killed him."

"And then he saved your life, how ironic." There was humor in the old man's voice.

"Yes, he saved my life. It was hard enough to stay aloof without that happening. The longer I spend with this boy the more I like him."

Olwin laughed at the seriousness in the small voice. "That must be difficult to admit." He bent down to the fire and lit a pipe he had pulled from his pocket. "Do the other colonies know about the boy?"

"I don't think so. None of them have showed up yet."

Olwin thought for a few minutes. "What will you do if he shows tendencies toward evil?" He watched the small dragon carefully.

"I will leave that decision to the Matriarch."

Olwin accepted the dragon's answer. "Then we will have to see to it that he shows none of those tendencies." Olwin stood and left the cavern.

Talon's first weeks as Olwin's apprentice were frustrating. After his short training with Graldiss, Talon felt he was past the rudimentary lessons Olwin was putting him through. He had spent two whole weeks moving objects around the cave, and four more moving *himself* around. The memory of slamming into a tree made Talon cautious at first. When his exasperation at the slow pace hit its limit Talon transported himself outside to the meadow.

Olwin immediately appeared next to him. "Lovely day. Now is a good time to study the special properties of plants." And he proceeded to point out the various flowers, roots and herbs; listing their properties and uses.

Talon's evenings were spent pouring over several dusty books, and listening to Graldiss and the old man argue over the finer points of weather directing, and the language of grass.

For the most part Graldiss sat and watched the training sessions, sometimes laughing at the complications wizards had made of doing simple tasks. On the few occasions Olwin went off on errands into the village or to visit other wizards, Graldiss taught Talon some words in Dragonese and recited many stories of dragon lore. Talon was glad of his company. He wasn't used to life as a hermit. The dragon was sorely missed when he returned home for short visits.

When Talon showed he was proficient at moving objects around the cave, Olwin took him outside and showed him a large, upright log. "Do you recall the first lesson I gave you?"

"Something about relocating people."

"Yes. Well why don't you give it a try." Olwin pointed to the log. "There's your victim."

Assuming that moving a large object was the same as moving anything else, Talon pictured the landing spot and "pushed". He was surprised to find himself sitting heavily on his backside. Olwin watched, straight faced. Talon concentrated harder, and landed harder. He didn't try a third time. "Ok, what am I doing wrong?" He rubbed his sore posterior. "I didn't have any trouble before."

The old wizard sat cross-legged on the grass. "Up until now you have only been working with light objects. I've been testing your strength by increasing the size. There is a finite amount of magic within each wizard. We draw on it for the mundane, daily magic. But to perform magic on a large scale, such as moving a 200 stone man, shifting a tornado, or fending off a hungry mountain lion, you will need to draw power from the elements around you."

Talon nodded, remembering how Graldiss had described magic to him.

"Feel the currents around you, breathe them in, absorb them through your pores, draw them up through the soles of your feet. Let it flow in, gather it up and focus its release. Slowly, don't take in more power than you need. Encompass the object you want moved, you don't want to rip it apart. Now release the thought in its entirety."

Talon concentrated, feeling the magic surge inside. His arms and legs tingled with power. He brought his hands up to encircle his view of the log; he saw a vague yellow glow between his palms. When he felt he had enough power to move the log he thrust his palm outward, arms straight. Talon wasn't prepared for the force that shot out through his hands. He was thrown back several feet. When the bark dust cleared he was pleased to see that the log was now on the other side of the meadow. He tried to stand, but his legs were weak and shaky.

Olwin nodded approvingly. "Not bad for your first try. How did it feel?"

Talon tried to answer, but found he had little breath for speech. It didn't matter; there were no words to describe how he felt. He just grinned.

"Yes, that's about how I felt, the first time. Now let me tell you what went wrong. Most noticeably, you didn't remember the advice given in the spell book: lean against something. When you are releasing that much energy there is always a backlash. It can push you a few inches, or a few feet. Always brace yourself. Second, and this will come with practice, you drew in more energy than needed for the task. If that log had been a man, he would have been blown apart. And when you draw in the power from objects around you, take only what they can give freely, too much can drain the life from the giver." Olwin pointed to the patch of ground Talon had stood on. The grass was brown and withered. "You must return any excess energy back to the giver. The edgy feeling you have is power residue. Come and give it back to the ground." Olwin knelt next to the darkened circle. Talon joined him. "Put your hands on the ground." Talon did as he was told. "Let some of your energy flow back. But be careful, some things are greedy and will feed off you until you are too drained to survive."

Talon felt an odd trickling run down his arms and out through his fingers. After a few minutes a feeling of warm thankfulness rose from the ground. Blades of grass became green again.

"Now thank the ground for the gift it has given."

Feeling a bit silly, Talon thanked the grass and dirt that still bore signs of his misuse.

Olwin helped Talon to his feet and transported them both to the warmth of the hearth. Talon thankfully accepted a mug of warm cider. "That was harder than I expected," he sighed.

Olwin chuckled but didn't make any comments. "Before you start moving people around, I suggest you practice on that log. When you can set it down gently and remain on your feet you can move on to living objects."

Talon and the log became close friends. During the next week they danced around the meadow. The dance was ungainly at first, like two repelling magnets. Talon would thrust and be thrust, but by the end of the week the log floated like a feather to be set gently wherever Talon chose. He soon discovered that by releasing a small amount of power behind him at the exact moment of thrust, he could stay on his feet. Talon found that he had to move around the meadow frequently during his hours of practice. The grass and ground at his feet began to anticipate his request for energy and started building up enough to keep him well supplied. For days his feet were burned by the intensity.

This was of some amusement to Graldiss, who was watching from a safe distance. "The ground is eager to get your lesson over with!" he called from a tree limb.

Talon didn't think it funny at all, and transported himself to the creek to cool his feet.

## Chapter 7

Early one morning Talon awoke at the sound of one of Olwin's cats hissing with indignation. He heard some soft mumbling in the larger cavern, but no light came down his passageway. He rolled over drowsily, thinking Olwin had returned from one of his trips and brought a friend. Moments later a bag was pulled roughly over his head and his hands were tied tightly together. He was dragged from the cave, and thrown onto the damp ground.

"He weren't no trouble at all, sir." A foot rudely rolled him over onto his face. "It was just as the sorc'r said, can't do no spells on us if he can't see us."

A wicked laugh answered the thug. Talon knew immediately that he lay at the feet of Rudrick Taldar. Thinking quickly, Talon spoke to the ground beneath him trying to leave a message for Olwin or Graldiss.

“I don't trust wizards.” Rudrick swung the hilt of his sword cruelly down on the covered head, knocking Talon unconscious. “Especially this one.”

Talon was picked up violently and thrown over the back of a horse. With some haste the party rode out of the meadow.

It was some hours before Talon came to. He kept very still, not wanting to receive another blow to his head. He took the direction of the party from the feel of the sun on his legs; he counted the number of horses from their hoof beats. From the idle conversation of his abductors Talon learned that Rudrick was not taking him to Precanlin, but some obscure village called Jessip. He was paying the thugs very well for their work, “easy money”. Rudrick was just a middleman, a sorcerer was behind the kidnapping and they didn't like working for a sorcerer, “untrustworthy types”. The thugs themselves had not seen the sorcerer, but they knew him from reputation. Talon had a pretty good idea Keldric was behind this.

They rode for hours in an easterly direction and soon entered a forest. They did not stop to eat or rest their horses. Talon's horse was growing tired. He picked up thoughts of aching bones, tired hooves and the certainty that there would *not* be a bag of warm oats at the end of the day. Talon sent kind thoughts to the horse, who appreciated that someone cared, and walked a bit smoother. Talon used a levitating spell to ease his weight from the horse's back. In grateful return, the horse, who said his owner called him Clod, but he preferred the human word Spring. The horse described in great detail the fancy-dressed man who had taken him from a comfortable farm and did not feed him nearly enough oats. Spring said that the mean man had bought him because his pack horse was lame. They had ridden four days, away from the waking sun. On the night of the round moon a man filled with magic joined them. The next day they walked to a dirty village with too many wagons. The man filled with magic left. Four sour-smelling men with mean horses joined them. Spring had thought he was going to have an adventure when he left the farm; free from the plow-thing that always followed behind him and the rats who left droppings in his oats. But it had been no adventure, until now.

"You are filled with magic," Spring said with some excitement. "You're clean, though, not like the one before, and you can hear me. I was worried at first, when I smelled dragon on you, but you don't act like one of *them*," he was relieved.

Talon smiled at Spring's observations. "That would be my friend you smell."

"Odd. I've never known dragons to associate with humans." Spring thought for a moment. "I don't think you are here freely."

"No, you are very observant. I'm sure this will not be a pleasant trip for me. The mean man, Rudrick, will probably turn me over to Keldric, the man with magic. Neither one likes me very much."

"But why are you still here? You are strong with magic."

"That may be, but they would just come after me again. Better to wait and find a way to deal with them permanently."

Spring let out a horse's laugh. "This may turn into an adventure after all."

"I'll do what I can. In the meantime, would you mind spreading the word of my capture to a few birds you see along the way? My name's Talon."

Talon sorted through what he had learned. He knew part of what Keldric had said was true, some of his ability was hindered by not being able to see his victims, but he had a few tricks up his sleeve. He knew the thugs were suspicious of Keldric; perhaps he could use this to his advantage. He also knew, if given the chance, Rudrick would not hesitate to kill him.

They rode on until past nightfall. Spring chatted on about his life on the farm, and let Talon know what kind of country they were riding through. When they stopped for the night Talon was thrown off Spring's back. He cried out when he hit the hard ground.

"Well now, awake, I see." Rudrick kicked Talon in the ribs. "That wizard said you had to be alive when we got to Jessip, but he didn't say we had to feed you."

Talon listened to the sounds of a fire being lit and food being prepared. He reached out for Spring, but he was happily chewing grass, and paying no attention. Well, if they weren't going to feed him, Talon felt no hesitation in making their evening miserable. He gathered the wind and blew out the fire. He spoke slowly to the trees and convinced them to drop a few of their precious cones near the heads of the offensive fire makers. Birds swooped down with the promise of bread.

It didn't take Rudrick long to decide who was to blame for their discomfort. With some pleasure, he clubbed Talon on the side of the head.

Talon woke with a headache. He was again being hoisted onto Spring's back. He made no noise or gave any indication that he was conscious. After they were on the move, Talon asked Spring about their surroundings.

"Still in the trees. It's nice and shady, but the flies are too thick. Did you have a nice sleep?"

"No, and there's a lump on my head to prove it."

They rode the rest of the morning in silence. Talon tried to reach the other horses, but their minds were dark and suspicious. They halted by a river. Rudrick grumpily paid to cross the bridge. They again rode all day, giving their horses little rest. When night fell they made camp near a stream.

"I know he must be awake by now," Talon heard Rudrick grunt. "Better club him again, so he doesn't give us any trouble."

Talon heard footsteps heading in his direction. He drew in energy from the rocks underneath him. He stiffened the cloth bag around his head until it was ridged. When the cudgel came down it solidly connected with the bag, leaving Talon's head safe for the night. The thug was satisfied with Talon's limp form. Talon didn't try any tricks on his captors that night.

The smell of roasting meat made Talon's stomach knot in agony. He was weakening with hunger. If he didn't do something about it soon, he would not be able to save himself later. The thoughts of a young mouse nearby gave him an idea. He asked the mouse if it would stand near to some of the food being prepared by the men. He couldn't *see* the food to transport it, but if he could get a picture from the mouse, he might be able to get a good estimation. The mouse happily cooperated and snuck up to a piece of bread. It let Talon know that just in front of his nose was a luscious treat. Talon allowed a few inches for the length of the mouse's nose, opened his mouth and relocated the piece of bread between his teeth. A wiggling lump of fur was not what he was hoping for. He apologized to the offended mouse, who escaped with a rude squeak. Exhausted and hungry, Talon slept.

The next morning Talon again stiffened the cloth around his head to keep from getting knocked out. Before they tossed him onto Spring, another horse entered the camp. Talon immediately knew the rider of this horse was a wizard.

"How is our guest?" Talon recognized Keldric's voice. Talon felt a probing of his thoughts, and easily blocked it.

"He tried some tricks the first night, but we've kept him knocked out since then." Rudrick answered cockily.

"I doubt that. He's conscious right now." Talon grunted when Keldric's staff struck his bent back. "But that won't matter now that I'm here." Keldric took hold of Talon's hand. "Where are the Rings?"

Talon did not answer. "He didn't have no rings on him," one thug offered.

"The old windbag must have them. That makes things easier. Let's get him to Jessip."

They rode on. Spring was forced to walk behind Keldric's stallion. "He smells," Spring complained.

By late morning they came out of the forest.

"What a nice grassy field," Spring commented. "I wish we would stop for a bite." Talon had to agree with him.

When there was room for the horses to walk abreast, Keldric slowed his horse to come alongside Spring. "I can feel the strength in you. Olwin has put a lot of work into you. Too bad he's wasted his time.

When I get you back to my manor I'll perform the Right of Transference. Your friend Taldar will be glad to assist with your death, though I'm sure he'll want to draw it out much longer than necessary. No matter, when you finally die I will take your power."

Spring slowed, worried at the dark thoughts from Talon. "I do not like this man." Spring said. "Would you like me to run away?"

"Thank you, friend, but they would only catch us and probably beat both of us. No, just follow along with them, for now."

Late in the afternoon Spring stopped suddenly. Something had frightened the horse. Spring's thoughts were too jumbled to read. Talon tried something he had seen in one of Olwin's books. Concentrating, he looked through Spring's eyes.

Dragons! The sky was filled with them! They dove at the smelly riders. The mean horses went wild, threw off their riders and ran into the woods. The smelly riders screamed like old women and huddled together, hiding their heads from the spurts of flames.

The fancy-dressed man yelled to the smelly men to get up and fight, but no one listened to him. A gigantic dragon swiped at the fancy-dressed man, who fell off his horse. The dragon lit the grass around the man on fire. Other dragons landed close by. The fancy-dressed man fell to his knees and began to cry and begged for mercy.

The magic man had gotten off his horse and stood defiantly cursing and shouting spells. Blue balls of light shot out of his hands at the dragons

Talon's bonds were cut. He pulled off the cloth bag from over his head. The light blinded him for a moment. He saw Rudrick and his men groveling on the ground. Keldric was waving his hands, throwing some kind of powder in the air.

Spring caught his attention: "Wow, look at them, I wish I could fly like that." Talon glanced Spring, and then followed its wondered gaze upwards. In his weakened state Talon lost his balance and fell to the ground.

Overhead a dozen dragons circled. Their colors glittered in the sunlight. Some swooped down on the cowering men, flaming above their heads. Others tried to roast Keldric, but found him shielded from their flames. Two reddish beasts conferred high in the sky, then one flew down toward the wizard. Talon looked away, not wanting to see Keldric fall prey to those immense jaws. There was a blood curdling scream, and the sound of Spring laughing, joined by the laughter of many of the dragons. Talon stood and turned around. A pile of steaming dragon dung stood where the mighty wizard had once been.

"Got his just deserts, I'd say." Talon turned in surprise at the sound of Graldiss' voice. The small dragon was flying from the direction of the forest. "Sorry to be late, can't seem to keep up like I used to." Talon laughed uncontrollably and clutched his small friend to his chest. The dragon wiggled out of Talon's grasp. "Control yourself, please, you'll ruin my reputation."

Talon stood and leaned on Spring. "I thought I was a goner. Are these friends of yours?" he asked Graldiss. "Please thank them for me," he said weakly.

A few dragons landed near Talon. "Are you sure this boy is worth saving?" asked one enormous brown dragon. "His power is very deep."

Graldiss stood resolutely in front of Talon. "This boy has the Matriarch's sanction." The surrounding dragons looked at Talon in awe and bowed their huge heads.

"Honored Child, what would you like us to do with your captors?"

Talon stared at the massive green face in front of his; it was much larger than Graldiss' had been when he was his full size. The blue swirled eyes were mesmerizing. A nip on his shoulder from Graldiss brought Talon back to the moment. He tried to think, he did not want to spend the rest of his life looking over his shoulder. But something must be done to deter Keldric from making a second attempt at abducting him. "Well, you could roast them slowly..." One of the cowering figures whimpered. Talon whispered something to Graldiss. "But," Talon said out loud, "we need to make an example of them."

Graldiss flew over the heads of the frightened men, and chanted softly. Slowly the hair on their heads began to turn snow white. By this time Keldric was beginning to crawl out from under the odorous pile. Graldiss mumbled at him as he flew past. The wizard disappeared in a theatrical puff of smoke.

Without another word, the dragons flew off, curious that the young wizard hadn't let them kill the offenders. Talon turned to Spring, "What would you like to do, my friend?"

Spring nuzzled Talon's arm. "You seem to be an interesting human. Perhaps I will stay with you for a while. I would be happy to carry you home, if you wish."

Talon nodded gratefully and mounted. The three rode off into the forest.

Once under the canopy of trees Talon looked back. His abductors had caught their horses and were riding hard in the opposite direction. "I'm so glad you found me," he said to Graldiss, who was making himself comfortable on Spring's neck.

"It wasn't hard, birds and trees have been babbling about it for the past day and a half." He stretched lazily. "One of my clutch-mates clued me in within a few hours of your abduction."

Talon pulled Spring to a halt. "Within a few hours?!" Remaining calm was not an option. He picked up the dragon by the scruff of the neck. "You knew what had happened to me within hours and you did nothing to help?!"

"Well you didn't appear to be in any danger." Graldiss explained lamely.

"No danger! I was clubbed, starved, kicked and carted off like a sack of turnips, and you say there was *no danger*?! I would like to hear your definition of danger." He dropped the dragon.

"The possibility of imminent dismemberment or death. Yes, I'll admit you were mistreated, but at no time was your life in peril. You heard Taldar, Keldric wanted you alive. And I noticed you found a way to protect yourself from that club. As for starving, there was nothing I could do about that without drawing suspicion. You yourself said if you escaped they would just come after you. We wanted to make sure they would never attempt such an act again, and for that we had to wait until you got out into the open."

Talon calmed down a bit at his friend's explanation. He could not fault anything Graldiss said. He rode in silence for some time. Spring babbled on about the excitement of the day, and how honored he was to have a real live dragon riding on his back. He would have something to tell the other horses when he returned to the farm.

"You don't have to go back there, if you don't want to," Talon said. "There's a wonderful meadow and a stream near our cave. You're welcome to stay as long as you'd like."

Spring was speechless.

Close to nightfall the small party made camp well into the woods. Graldiss lit a fire and caught Talon a rabbit. When they were settled for the night, Talon asked Graldiss about Keldric. "Why was he waiting to kill me? Why not just let Rudrick have his fun right there and take my power right away?"

"You are apprenticed to Olwin. If you had died there in the field, Olwin would have been alerted immediately and would have been drawn to your body. Keldric didn't want to deal with the old man, so he needed to get to his chambers where he could set up a shield around you. And then, if Olwin had showed up, Keldric would have the upper hand. It is always an advantage to fight on your own territory."

"What did you do to Keldric that made him so upset?"

Graldiss chuckled, "I just touched up his hair a bit, like the others." Talon didn't get the joke. "Haven't you noticed wizards have white hair and beards? Most of them are quite proud of their length, and Keldric was no exception. I thought, since your abductors were going to have to live with new hair color, Keldric should have to as well. I'm sure his theatrics won't be as dramatic with long *black* hair." Talon had to agree, and laughed.

"I'm curious, why didn't Keldric translocate from under that pile of dung?"

"Oh, haven't you heard? Dragon dung blocks magic. Quite often villagers come and clear out our caves. I think they spread the stuff on their roofs. I'd hate be around after a good rain."

The next morning Talon's strength was restored enough for him to transport himself and Spring to the meadow below the cave. Graldiss joined them. Spring was thrilled with this new method of travel and happily frolicked in the wild flowers. A few days later Olwin returned from town. He looked tired. Talon thought it best not to tell his mentor of his latest adventures.

During the following weeks of training; Talon focused on skills that would serve him if he were ever held captive again. He practiced sensing objects while blindfolded and moving them around the cave, including himself.

Graldiss tried to explain to Talon this was all unnecessary. In a few months he would be a full wizard and no one, not even Keldric, would be able to pull off such an outrageous plan again.

Talon had his doubts, especially remembering the look on Keldric's face before he left that field. Better to be prepared for anything. Next time he might not have a horde of dragons around to rescue him.

## Chapter 8

The first day of autumn was damp but warm. Talon brooded in front of the fire, the prospect of spending the coming winter in the confining cave was not to his liking. Graldiss was scratching contentedly at his hind leg. He had begun molting the day before, and a dusting of shed dragon-scale dander covered the hearth. The changing season effected Olwin the most; he struggled to get out of bed in the mornings, ate less at meal-times, and was more distracted with his research. Talon was worried about the old man's condition. The Rings of Ko-Mon Po had helped his health in the beginning, but now made little difference.

This morning Olwin seemed to be having a conversation with himself as he ate breakfast. Talon wondered if senility was beginning to set in. When the conversation began to get animated Talon thought it safer to leave the room. He didn't want to get hit with a flying potion-pot this early in the day.

Outside the cave Talon sat on an outcrop, dangling his legs. He listened to the chatter of anxious squirrels and bragging sparrows. A lone puff of cloud drifted overhead. Talon stretched out his mind. "Good morning little cloud."

"Who is that?" The voice in Talon's mind sounded young and frightened.

"I'm a friend, down here on the ground."

"Have you seen my family? I stopped to watch a hawk and can't find them." Talon could hear panic setting in.

Talon sent his thoughts out as far as he dared. He finally found a flock of ducks that had just flown through a bank of clouds. One motherly duck had noticed a feeling of loss from one particularly large cloud which was trying to keep track of a number of smaller clouds. Talon thanked the duck and returned his mind to the meadow. With a calm word and a gentle push Talon sent the lost cloud on its way.

"Talking to clouds, now?" Graldiss chuckled. "I suppose they're more interesting than...grass. You're getting better at muffling your releases."

Talon shrugged, "Practice makes perfect."

"Well not perfect, yet. But you may make it before you're a hundred."

Talon grunted and turned away. He wasn't in the mood for the dragon's humor and he didn't like being reminded his life was now going to span many times that of ordinary people. He had put this thought out of his mind. As a soldier, Talon had come to accept the inevitability of death. Now the road of his life was stretching out without any clear ending. The only sure thing in his life, death, had been taken away from him. No, that wasn't exactly true; Olwin was dying, wasn't he. Talon stood and returned to the cave.

Talon expected to see the old man asleep by the fire; instead, Olwin was bustling around the cave, stuffing various items into a heavy cloth traveling bag.

"Going someplace?" Talon asked.

"Where have you been? Didn't you hear me call? Yes, we're going someplace. Pack what you'll need for a few weeks stay."

Talon had grown used to the old man being obscure and went to pack. Graldiss was not so accepting.

"What bug has gotten into his cotton-filled head? This is not the time of the year to start gallivanting around the countryside." He warmed his shiny new scales in front of the fire. "This must have something to do with the chat he was having this morning." Talon looked blankly at his friend. "Sounded like he was talking to Barkin." Talon was still in the dark. "Hasn't the old goat told you about the other wizards?"

Talon shook his head. He *had* thought it odd that Olwin had never mentioned others of their kind, but

Talon had put it off to his general dislike of the other wizards.

Graldiss sighed noisily. “He and Keldric aren't the only wizards around you know. Barkin is fairly innocuous, spends his time dissecting corpses and figuring out how humans work. Imlay has been having a conversation with a mountain for several centuries. Fernley roams around with a band of minstrels, seems he likes to play the lute. And Poldrun has been training a long line of kings. There are others out there, but they don't cause enough trouble for us to make a fuss about. We spend most of our time keeping tabs on the likes of Keldric, Oret and Gildex. Those three are best kept at a great distance. They're power hungry and kill dragons to absorb their magic. They and their predecessors were the cause of our near extinction. Be careful of them. They are not above killing a wizard or apprentice for his magic, as you know from your experience with Keldric.”

Talon hurried with his packing. “If this Barkin knows human anatomy he may be a healer, too. I'm surprised Olwin has waited this long to go see him.”

Graldiss puffed the fire ablaze. “I'm surprised he's going *now*. I'm sure you've noticed that wizards aren't very companionable people. They're even worse around their own kind, very competitive, so I've heard. After a few ales it's dangerous to be anywhere in the vicinity of a pair of wizards. There have been more than a few major battles between disagreeing factions. Not a pretty sight. No, the old man must be pretty bad to be going for a second opinion."

Talon thought about this while he finished packing. As he went to join Olwin, Talon looked back at the snoozing dragon, "Are you going to come along?"

Graldiss opened one eye, "I think it'll be best if I stay here and keep the home fires burning. I don't want it to be general knowledge that we can be shrunk like a pair of wool socks." He closed his eye and rolled over.

Talon and Olwin walked silently through the damp meadow. At the main road a wagon was waiting for them. The driver was nervously looking up and down the road.

"Logan," Olwin greeted the man.

"Sir." The driver was dressed in worn, dusty clothes and sat stiffly.

"How is Gertrude doing?"

The man seemed to relax a bit at the question. "Much better, thanks to you. The potion you gave her put her right back on her feet."

"Does she still complain at milking?"

The man's smile showed many missing teeth. "Indeed, sir. Especially as the mornings get colder. I should have had you bring something for her temper.

Why just the other day she kicked me just 'cause I didn't let her go through the gate first."

"She has a mean streak. I'm surprised you've put up with her for so long."

"Oh, in her early years, she was quite friendly, nuzzled up to me all the time. Now she's just an obstinate old cow."

Olwin climbed in the back of the wagon. "You should take a switch to her when she forgets who the boss is."

Talon was surprised at the old man's comment. He climbed carefully into the rickety wagon.

"Thought had occurred to me, sir, but I don't have the heart." Logan pulled out onto the road. "If the roads aren't too muddy we'll be in Needam just after nightfall."

Talon quickly sat next to Olwin as the wagon began to move, and pulled a bundle of fresh-smelling hay behind him. "Not a very good example of marital bliss," he commented softly.

Olwin laughed, "Marital bliss? Gertrude isn't Logan's wife, she's his *cow*."

Talon watched as the old man laughed himself into a coughing fit.

After an hour in the swaying, bumping wagon Talon was sure he could get to Needam faster on foot. He stuffed hay behind his back and under his legs to pad against the rough wood. To make the ride worse, it began to rain.

Olwin seemed heedless of the moisture and dropped off to sleep. Logan whistled a rambling tune; his floppy hat shielded him from the drizzle. Talon sat miserably. He attempted to divert the drops magically, but was having little luck; there was just too many of them. He pulled up his collar and resigned himself to a thorough drenching.

It was well past sundown before the muddy wagon and its soggy passengers arrived at a wide, one-level house on the outskirts of the village of Needam. Talon was thankful *this* wizard chose to live like a civilized man and looked forward to a warm bath to wash away the smell of wet hay.

A young, well-dressed man greeted them at the door. He showed them to comfortable rooms and informed them that Master Barkin was in town and would return in the morning. After a hot soak and a change of dry clothes, Talon joined Olwin in the sitting room. An ample supper had been laid on a side table and a fire was crackling merrily.

"I've talked to Barkin about you. He's agreed to teach you some of what he knows while I'm searching his library," Olwin said between slurps of soup. "We'll be here a few weeks at the least."

"Then he won't be trying to cure you?"

Olwin turned to look at Talon. "I'm past that stage now, I'm afraid. I'll let him look me over, I suppose. He may be able to tell me the course the illness will run. But what I really came for was a chance to look through his library."

This was the first time Talon had heard Olwin speak about his illness with such finality. It worried him so he changed the subject. "Graldiss said wizards are competitive. Is that why I haven't met any others?"

Olwin smiled. "I suppose the beast is right in some ways, we don't have get-togethers to swap spells. But most of us help each other out in a pinch. We tend to specialize in our use of magic so some sharing of information is necessary. Yes, there have been rivalries and there are things I would rather not let my brothers-in-magic know that I have learned. It's not as dramatic as I'm sure Graldiss made it out to be. As for meeting other wizards, there has been little need of that up until now. Your dragon and I have taught you everything you need to know. When I die you will receive the sum total of all my knowledge and that should fill in most of the gaps."

"Why is Barkin's library so special?"

Olwin shrugged, "After my own collection, Barkin's is the most complete. There are still things about you and your power that puzzle me. I hope to find some answers here. And I suppose there are a few things Barkin can teach you that I haven't mastered." Olwin rose and turned to the door. "The bed in my room looked extravagantly soft. I think I'll indulge myself with a good night's sleep."

Talon retired to his own room, and sunk into his own soft mattress. He could hear the old man's snores through the wall. The strain of the day seemed to flow out of Talon and he was soon fast asleep.

A gentle tap on the door roused Talon from sleep. The servant he met last night opened the door "Good morning, sir, I am Jossa. If you need anything, please don't hesitate to ask."

While the neatly dressed servant busied himself laying out breakfast Talon studied him unnoticed. Jossa was small and slightly built. He did not hold himself with the erectness of the upper class, but made himself smaller so as not to draw attention to himself. Though his clothes were perfectly tailored, Jossa did not look comfortable in them. The young man's hair was the only natural part of his appearance. It was an unruly mop of black curls. Talon smiled when they fell across the solemn eyes.

Jossa pulled back the curtains. "Master Barkin bids you to break your fast and meet him in his study at your leisure."

Talon sat up slowly. "Has Olwin risen?"

Jossa spread out Talon's cleaned clothes onto a chair. "Master Olwin rose some hours ago and is currently in conference with Master Barkin. Is there anything else you wish?"

Talon shook his head. "No, thank you." Jossa shut the door quietly. Talon slid off the bed, he felt oddly refreshed. He had never slept in such a soft bed before. He dressed quickly and devoured the meal set before the fire. When he made his way downstairs Jossa was waiting and showed Talon quietly into the study.

Olwin was putting his shirt on while a well-dressed man with a short-cropped white beard busily wrote down notes. He referred frequently to an old scroll. "I would have to say your own observations are probably correct. If you had gotten the Rings earlier it may have made a difference. I'm amazed at the subtlety; I'm surprised you discovered it at all. This was not the work of a novice. You had to have come in contact with the culprit, too. This sort of thing could not have been done from any distance."

Olwin nodded. "I have my suspicions. We were all quite cozy at Micca's Transference a few years back. There was enough energy floating around that a spell of this magnitude would not have been noticed."

"The only ones capable of this kind of work would be Poldrun, Oret, Keldric, and of course, myself."

Olwin thought a moment. "Poldrun was injured and didn't come to the Transference. Oret would have left his fingerprints all over the place, he's never been known for his subtlety."

Barkin laughed. "No, his style generally includes bolts of lightning, herds of elephants, or carnivorous purple flowers. Have you considered the Dragons? Any one of them could have pulled this off, even at a distance."

"No, I've always stayed on the right side of *them*. My money's on Keldric. We've never been on good terms, and he came to visit me shortly before I sent for the Rings. Some pretense about a spell for wind running. Now that I think of it, he was rather curious about my health. He would give a room full of gold to obtain my power. Well it's a moot point now, the Rings have broken the spell but the damage is done. I have an apprentice who will receive my power when the time comes." Olwin turned to Talon.

Barkin took notice of Talon for the first time. He stood and went to greet the boy. "Welcome. I hope you slept well."

Talon nodded. "Yes, thank you. It was the best night of sleep I've had in a very long time." Talon noticed for the first time how young Barkin was. His hair was white, of course, but his face was unlined and youthful.

"It took me quite a while to come up with just the right blend of spells to induce a good night's rest." Barkin held out his hand. "I'm very pleased to meet you, Talon. From what Olwin says, you have quite a talent."

Talon looked quickly at Olwin. The barely perceptible nod of the old man's head told Talon that Barkin didn't know the whole story. "It's been hard work plowing through the spell books Olwin makes me study," Talon said with a laugh. "But it's easier than a winter's siege."

Barkin nodded and showed Talon to the overstuffed chair close to the desk. "Olwin told me you were a mercenary. The lack of political alliance may prove in your favor. Poor Poldrun can't see past his fancy robes and title." He lit a thin cigar. "Olwin has asked me to teach you what I can about the use of magic within the human body. It is unusual for one wizard's apprentice to be taught by another. But the time constraints in these circumstances may allow for a little bending of the rules." He looked deep into Talon's eyes. "Is it *your* wish to learn what I have to teach?"

Under the strength of Barkin's stare Talon had the uncomfortable feeling that he could only speak the truth. "I do not know what use such knowledge would be." He tore his eyes from Barkin's. "But I will be led by Olwin's wisdom."

Barkin thought for a moment, and then nodded. "A worthy answer. While Olwin browses through my library, I will teach you." He stood, a gentle wave of power brushed past Talon. The door opened and

Jossa entered. "Take this young man to the work room, I will join him momentarily."

Talon followed the silent back of the servant and was led to the rear of the house. They passed through an antechamber with rows of benches, then into a bright room with a single table in the center of the stone floor. Racks of strange instruments lined one short wall, books lined the opposite. Jossa pulled down the end of a large parchment scroll that covered the empty wall. After a moment Talon recognized the intricate picture to be of the human body, the skin was left off though, showing the contours of muscles, tributaries of veins, snake-like intestines, and a lot of disgusting blobs.

"Master Barkin will want you to study this chart. There are small numbers on the individual components with corresponding annotations along the side of the parchment." Jossa left Talon staring at the grotesque illustration.

Talon took a deep breath. He started with something familiar. He had seen many arm and shoulder wounds in battle. He recognized some of the names of the bones and muscles from the overheard conversations of the doctors. Tongue-twisting names of muscles and veins boggled his mind. Morbid interest soon drew Talon's eyes to the disgusting blobs. He followed the maze of the intestine to its end, and shifted uncomfortably. Talon stepped back. He thought it might be best to get an overall impression before getting too engrossed in the particulars. His strategic mind soon saw patterns in the path of the veins, in the joints and connections of muscles.

"One must get the lay of the land before building a plan of attack," he said with determination.

Talon was making headway when Barkin entered the room. "Someone must have spent a lot of time cutting up people to get this much detail," Talon noted.

Barkin smiled, he was glad this boy would not be squeamish around him. He had had a difficult time finding people that didn't cringe and turn green over the simplest conversations. Even if the population of Needam gladly received his medical ministrations, they not-too-secretly thought Barkin too morbid for polite company.

"Let's start with a basic lesson in the anatomical workings of the human body."

The "basic" lesson took many hours. Talon hardly noticed that they had worked through the mid-day meal, or Jossa coming in to light the lamps. It was only when Olwin came in search of them that he realized how late it had become.

"The duck is getting cold." Olwin called from the doorway. "And please refrain from any discussion of bodily fluids and the workings of my innards.

"Only if you promise not to bore me with your histories." Barkin followed the old man to the dining room.

The rest of the evening Talon sat quietly, listening to the two powerful men trade stories. While he dozed before the fire body parts haunted his mind. Skeletal warriors battled skinless enemies, each naming body parts they cut from each other. At some unknown hour Talon felt wrapped in energy and moved to his bed. Happily, his anatomical nightmares subsided with the move.

The days settled into an easy routine. Talon ate a solitary breakfast, studied with Barkin until mid-day, and then read Barkin's journals until supper. Talon learned how to ease a man's pain, redirect the flow of blood from a wound, and find and remove a clot inside the brain. He memorized spells for gout, aching joints, hair loss and foot fungus. He practiced listening to the body itself to find the cause of an ache or pain. Using animal cadavers, Talon practiced reattaching severed nerves, muscles, and bones. Barkin taught Talon to *see* within the body, to heal without having to cut the body open.

Some days Talon would be allowed to observe Barkin treating some of the townsfolk. It was only on these occasions that Talon saw Barkin wear anything but his neat, fashionable suits. When he saw patients Barkin wore a stylized wizard's robe, blue and plain, no hood or high collar, and sleeves that stopped at the elbows. When Talon asked him about it, Barkin explained that he had never found the robes comfortable, but his patients seemed to expect him to wear them. He had these made so that they would not interfere with the task at hand.

During one of Talon's visits to the clinic he learned Jossa was not just Barkin's house servant, he also assisted in the medical clinic, dispensing potions and herbs, clarifying written directions, calming waiting patients, and even handling some of the less drastic medical cases. One evening Talon asked Jossa if he was Barkin's apprentice.

A look of astonishment flooded the young man's face. "Why, sir, I could never aspire to such heights. I am a simple servant, nothing more."

Talon put a calming arm on Jossa's shoulder. "You don't have to be anyone special to apprentice to a wizard. I was a soldier before Olwin decided to take over my life."

Jossa looked kindly at the boy. "Even a soldier is above my position in life. I was given to Master Barkin as payment for services." He said no more and Talon didn't bring it up again.

One morning, when Barkin was out calling on a patient, Talon went in search of Olwin. Every day the old man would wish him good morning, and then disappear into Barkin's library. Curiosity finally got the best of Talon, and he quietly opened the thick oak doors he had seen Olwin pass through.

Talon thought it odd that the room was so dark. Every other room in the house was brightly lit with windows and oil lamps; the library seemed to have neither. The only light seemed to be coming from glowing orbs hanging in the corners of the ceiling. Talon had often seen the cavern that held Olwin's collection of books, and there was no doubt that Barkin's collection was larger. Each of the four walls was lined floor to high-ceiling with book-filled shelves. Row upon row of tightly packed shelves filled the room, the spaces between them only wide enough for a man to pass without brushing the spines of the ancient volumes.

Talon slowly walked into the silent room. He passed by dry cracking spines with titles in some unknown language. One book caught his eye; the binding and covers were of a rough reddish material, the writing on the spine was gold. Talon reached out and put his hand on the ancient volume. He was surprised at the heat under his fingertips. In horror, Talon pulled his hand away; the book's binding was dragon hide! He shivered and moved quickly down the aisle. He followed the sound of muffled mumbling and turning pages until he located his mentor.

"You know, I don't think it's healthy to be shut away in a place like this." Talon commented.

"You choose your entertainment, I'll choose mine." Olwin scribbled some notes, then closed the book and returned it to the shelf, pulling out the next book. "How are your studies going? Sliced up anyone today?"

Talon ignored the remark. "It's refreshing to work with someone who's organized and methodical." He peered over the old man's shoulder at the book. The words on the yellowed parchment made no sense, and they seemed to move around the thick pages. He shook his head to clear the dizziness. "I could study for years and not learn everything Barkin could teach me."

"That's not surprising, since it took centuries for him to learn what he knows. He's trained many Normals in the healing arts, though it will be a while before he's ready to take an apprentice."

"Barkin's more powerful than he appears." Talon brushed his fingers absently along a book's spine. His mind was filled with a sudden flash of panic. He had an irrational need to run away. They were coming after him. He wouldn't let them lock him up again. They would pay for what they did...with blood.

Olwin laid a hand on Talon's shoulder and whispered a spell. Talon felt the hatred drain from his mind and return to the book. "Be careful what you touch. Books have a mind of their own. Their knowledge can seep into your head without your realizing it."

Talon wiped his hand across his eyes. He took a breath and collected his thoughts. "You're spending a lot of time in here. What are you looking for?"

"Oh, just filling in some gaps," Olwin said evasively. "Different perspectives from different authors."

Talon knew the old man was being purposely vague. He looked around and conversationally observed: "This is quite a collection. When does Barkin find time to read all these books?"

"The man's not as young as he appears," Olwin said, not lifting his eyes from the faded page. "You can fit a lot into two centuries. Now was there something you wanted to speak to me about, or are you just in the mood to annoy me?"

"I just wanted to make sure you were still alive. You spend so much time in here I thought you may have been swallowed up by an encyclopedia of carnivorous snails."

Olwin laughed and pulled down a dusty scroll. "Will you leave me alone if I promise to make an appearance at supper?"

"If you aren't sitting at the dining table in an hour I'll assume that the encyclopedia got you and have Jossa come to clean up the remains." He left the oblivious old man to his books.

Three weeks after their arrival, Olwin announced at supper they had imposed on Barkin's hospitality long enough, and would be returning home the next morning.

Talon accepted this news with both disappointment and cheer. He knew there was so much more to learn from Barkin, but he missed his conversations with Graldiss and even looked forward to his own uncomfortable bed.

Talon felt honored when Barkin offered him a slim volume of medical spells. "You have great potential, boy. Now that our minds have touched you may call on me at any time for assistance." Talon was speechless.

"Come visit sometime," Olwin offered as they departed.

"You know I'll see you again soon." They clasped hands.

Talon was thankful for the well-sprung wagon Olwin had hired to carry them back to Arklin. The speed of the horses was also a good sign. The only drawback was the lumpiness of the bags of turnips.

"Well, boy, I hope your time was well spent," Olwin said conversationally.

"It's an interesting field of study; I may look into it further in a few years."

"Never cared for mucking about with people's innards. Leave them on the inside where they belong." Olwin said with a grimace.

It was late at night before the wagon pulled into the courtyard of the Hen and Hound. After paying the wagon driver Olwin transported himself and Talon to the entrance of their cave. They walked silently into the main cavern. They both stopped at the sight of a dozen cats lounging by the fire, and one contented dragon in their midst. It was good to be home.

## Chapter 9

Graldiss' rough shaking startled Talon. "Wake up!" He had slept little that night and was irritated at the rude awakening. "They're here!" Graldiss shouted. "Dress quickly!" and he rushed out of the cave. Talon had no idea who the beast was talking about. They weren't expecting visitors. While he dressed, Talon felt an oppressive weight around him and longed for a cup of tea.

Graldiss wasn't in the main cavern. Olwin was taking his time getting out of bed, so Talon walked toward the cave entrance alone. He stopped in mid-step; someone was probing into his mind. He tried to *feel* the wizard on the other end, but was hit with a powerful mental blast that made his head spin.

"Don't be impertinent, boy," a large voice boomed in his head. "My mind is not for your scrutiny,"

"You started it," Talon said vocally. He really needed that cup of tea.

Talon paused at the cave's entrance, letting his eyes adjust to the bright sunlight. Although he didn't know who had arrived uninvited, Talon expected his usual view of the meadow and fir-lined mountain. He got neither. An enormous mottled-orange hide obscured his entire view. He stepped back and looked up.

The dragon standing before him did not look like any he had seen before. The nose of the tremendous beast was comparatively small and the teeth in the grinning jaws were less vicious-looking. Massive golden horns curled in a tight spiral from ear to jaw. Gentle eyes of the lightest blue Talon had ever seen, stared deeply into his. There was no doubt this magnificent creature had looked into his thoughts a moment ago. He knew instinctively this was no ordinary dragon.

Talon's mind raced to think of what he should do. Diplomacy was always the best option. He bowed low. "I am truly honored to be in the presence of so noble a beast. To what do I owe this privilege?"

The silence was thick. Talon's perfect use of Dragonese had surprised the mass of dragons he now noticed gathered in the meadow, but pleased the massive figure before him.

"We have been watching your progress, young Talon. I felt that it was time to pay you a visit."

Olwin shuffled out of the cave, a cup of tea in his hand. He didn't seem surprised at all by the presence of the magnificent orange dragon at his doorstep or the multitude of dragons in his meadow. "I don't suppose you considered timing your visit a bit later in the day, Magrid? No, you would have lost the element of surprise and the effect of a hoard of dragons shining in the sunrise." He took a sip of tea. "I would invite you in for breakfast, but you'd probably break my best chair."

Graldiss was beside himself at Olwin's insulting behavior, and tried to stammer out an apology. The Matriarch brushed him aside. "Please, don't delay your morning meal on my account." Talon felt a soft rush of energy and the cave ledge was suddenly furnished with Olwin's table (breakfast beautifully laid out), two chairs and a stool with one of Olwin's cats snoozing, oblivious, upon it.

Olwin laughed and bowed to the majestic dragon. "Would you care for a cup of tea?" He took a seat at the table and buttered a slice of toast. "I didn't expect you for a month or so. Has he advanced that far already?"

Magrid tossed the contents of the tiny cup of tea into her mouth. "The time is near for both you and the boy." She speared a slice of toast with a dainty claw.

Talon watched the ridiculous scene of the old wizard and dragon matriarch dining together as if they were great friends. He was annoyed at being spoken about. "Bacon?" he offered irritably. "Since I seem to be the subject of this conversation, care to include me?"

The Matriarch looked at Talon. "If you are as smart as our small brother claims you are, I'm sure you know we've been interested in you for some time. You are coming to the end of your training as a wizard. There is still much at stake, and I am here to pass judgment on you, personally."

He searched his memory for comments Graldiss had made about the dragons keeping an eye on him, but he could not remember anything that indicated he was as important as the Matriarch implied. "I'm sorry, I must be slow this morning, and I don't understand why you are so interested in me. From what Olwin has told me, my ability to use magic is unique, and I understand my relationship with Graldiss is unusual for a dragon and wizard, but it hardly merits this attention."

Magrid looked at Olwin, the old man shrugged. "I didn't want him distracted. His ego is already inflated. I thought there was still enough time to prepare him."

"Enough time? Are you telling me a powerful wizard such as yourself hasn't divined the time of your own passing?" Olwin looked away sheepishly. "That is your own business, but the boy is not. If he is to take his place in The Great Pattern, he will have to be told everything." The massive head turned to look at Talon. "Sit down, young man." Talon did as he was told.

The great dragon sat back on her haunches and looked into Talon's eyes, a low hum came from the multitude gathered in the meadow. "Legends and prophecies have told of the coming of a leader, the Krrig Daa, who would be a bridge between our two species; to bring an end to the hostilities and bring forth a new age of magic. For centuries we looked for that leader, but he never came. Sixteen years ago certain prophecies were fulfilled that indicated the arrival of the Chosen One who would lead us into the new age. Still we looked no further than our own caves for his presence. We were wrong to make that assumption."

A sick feeling grew in the pit of Talon's stomach. He mechanically took a bite of bread.

"Early last year your power came to the attention of two brothers." The crowd of dragons shouted the names of Felgrig and Tolago. "We were lucky they did not kill you on the spot. I sent a young student to watch you." Graldiss blushed when his name was shouted by his fellow dragons. "His reports fueled the hope that you might indeed be the one we had been waiting for. When he returned to us after your rescue of him from the clutches of Keldric, The Wicked," a rumbling growl rose from the listening crowd, "I knew our searching was over."

Talon stood abruptly, "No, you're wrong, I'm not the one you're looking for." Olwin put his hand on the boy's arm. Talon shook free. "I'm nothing special, don't you understand that?" He ran into the cave.

Graldiss flew after him. He found Talon stuffing clothes into his old pack.

"I'm not the one you're all looking for. You know there's nothing special about me." Talon jammed a shirt into the pack for emphasis.

"'Alone He will come,'" the small dragon intoned, "'and the earth will give Him power. He will know the ways of men, and plot against them. The mightiest will be reduced before Him. And through Him the rift will be healed.'"There was a long pause. Talon sat heavily on his bed. "Accept who you are." Graldiss said unsympathetically.

"I don't know who I am anymore" Talon sighed heavily. "A year ago I knew who I was, a young mercenary with a knack for battle tactics. I trained hard, fought where I was told and planned the deaths of hundreds of young men just like me. That's who I was. Now I'm what you, an old man, and now a dragon queen, say I am. I don't know if I like what you've made me."

"So you'd rather be a mercenary? Fine," Graldiss said angrily, "I'll see that you are paid handsomely to protect my race." He left without looking back.

Talon stared after his friend. His first instinct was to go after him, but what could he say? He sat heavily on his bed and buried his face in his hands.

"Don't worry, he'll cool off soon."

Talon looked up. Olwin was standing in the doorway, a bright orange cat weaving between his legs. "This is my fault, I'm sorry. I should have told you long ago."

"Is it really true?" Talon held out one last ray of hope that this was all a mistake.

"Yes," the old man said quietly.

"How long have you known?"

"Shortly after you returned with the Rings, my suspicions about your abilities drew me to my history books, and later Barkin's library. The only reference about inborn power led me to the prophecies Magrid spoke of. The method you used to save Graldiss left no doubt: 'The mightiest will be reduced', how else do you explain what you did to Graldiss?" Olwin sat next to Talon, the orange cat leaped onto Talon's lap. "I didn't tell you then because you were hardly able to handle the idea of being a wizard. You must admit you would have run far and fast if I had told you that you were destined to save the dragon race. I focused on your training instead. You might have been the chosen one, but they would not have hesitated to kill you if you showed any signs of becoming a dark wizard."

Talon turned at this news.

“We had to be sure of you.” These thoughts came from the cat lounging on his lap. It grinned up at him. “Many good men turned toward evil with the power you have. Scratch me behind my ears,” Magrid ordered imperially.

“And I wasn’t told any of this.” Talon said flatly, absently scratching the ‘cat’.

“What would you have done with this knowledge?” the cat asked.

Talon couldn’t answer and decided to change the subject. “She said your time was near,” he said to the old man. “What did she mean?”

Olwin was silent.

The cat looked sadly up at Talon “I meant that he would die before the next full moon. Silly of him not to be keeping track of something so important. I have *my* passing down to the final minutes.”

“Yes, and I bet you color coordinate your rubies and emeralds, too. Knowing makes the wait seem longer, so I choose not to dwell on the matter. I know the end is close and have begun to make final arrangements, if that makes you happy.”

The cat flipped its tail unimpressed.

Talon looked into the future they had revealed to him and felt inadequate. “I don’t know if I can do what you’re asking. I’m trying to be realistic about this. Less than a year ago I didn’t believe in magic *or* dragons and now I’m going to be this...Krrig Daa? I can’t even transport across a meadow without slamming into a tree," he exaggerated. "I'm too new at this."

Magrid curled under Talon's chin. "The very fact that you are hesitant is a good sign. When the time comes, you will find the knowledge and courage you need."

This should have made Talon feel better, but it didn't.

Talon followed Olwin and the orange cat outside. Magrid transformed smoothly, her energy-release was barely perceptible. She spoke softly to Graldiss, and then turned to the assembled dragons. "This young boy has accepted his fate. I give him my blessing." The multitude cheered. The mighty orange dragon turned to Talon. "Be well, we will speak again soon. Trust what is in your heart." With a mighty heave of her rear legs, she thrust herself into the air; her magnificent wings unfurled and with great sweeping motions Magrid, Matriarch of Dragons, flew into the clouds. Dozens of dragons followed, others simply disappeared. Only the small figure of a horse stood dazed in the deserted meadow.

Talon sagged against the cave entrance. "What a way to start a morning." He looked at Graldiss, who seemed in a trance. "I'm sorry about the way I acted. Something like this ought to be broken to a person slowly."

The small dragon slumped against Talon's leg. "Well, imagine what is was like for me, finding out your best friend is the savior of your race."

Olwin transported the dining table back into the cave. "Come on, let's finish breakfast."

The next weeks were filled with intense training. Talon had once thought of Olwin's magic as petty and simplistic; but now it was easy to see there was much more to this odd old man's power than met the eye. Each night Talon fell into bed, too exhausted to think to about the future. Each new day brought with it new aspects of his talent.

Talon began to notice Olwin was growing weaker with each passing day. The realization that his mentor would not be around much longer made the training sessions more important. The moment Talon dreaded was fast approaching. A friend was going to die and he would be left alone to stumble into his destiny.

Olwin's end came sooner than Talon expected. Early one morning Olwin lay motionless in his bed. "No lessons today, boy," he said wearily. "I've taught you all I can." The tired eyes closed, the silence was broken only by the old man's labored breath.

Talon went to the hearth to brew a cup of healing tea, his whole body trembled. His mind was caught between paralysis and urgency. He stumbled around trying to mix the tonic, struggling to think clearly, spilling ingredients on the floor.

A weak moan drew Talon's attention back to Olwin. He leaned down to hear his words. "The Rings." Olwin tried to lift his hand. "Take the Rings."

Talon shook his head. "No, you still need them."

Olwin's head rolled limply back and forth. "They have fulfilled their purpose. They have allowed me to live long enough to see you able to take my place. Take them." His eyes slowly closed.

Talon did as he was told, and slid them onto his own thumbs. They tingled as he'd remembered. Now he felt their full power surging through him. He looked down at Olwin. The loss of the Rings seemed to deflate him somehow.

Talon held Olwin's fragile hand in his. He knew the old man would not be waking up. He had done everything he could to ease Olwin's pain, but he still had much to learn about medicinal magic. He hoped he had done enough.

Olwin's cats must have known the end was near; they gathered around the bed, huddled close to the still body and began to purr. Talon would have shooed them away, but the smile on the dying man's lip forestalled him. Olwin took a final deep breath, through his pale lips he whispered: "We will meet again soon." Then he sighed, as if it were a relief to let go of life. The cats lifted their heads in unison and let out a mournful yowl. Graldiss joined them. Talon felt tears roll down his cheeks.

Later that night Graldiss watched Talon from the fireplace mantle. He didn't know how to comfort his friend. Humans had such confusing ideas about death. They grieved at the loss of the body rather than to rejoice at the freeing of the spirit. Didn't Talon know Olwin would be with him always? Hadn't the old man told him about the Transference? The dragon thought back to the last few weeks, and couldn't remember hearing the two of them talking about what would happen in the next 24 hours following Olwin's death. Talon's reaction definitely indicated that he thought his mentor was lost to him forever. The foolish old man! He had left it to Graldiss to show Talon the way. And Graldiss had preparations of his own to make. Humans!

"Come boy, put aside your pain. We have work to do."

Talon watched Graldiss jump down beside him and looked away. "Leave me alone."

Graldiss whipped Talon's ankle with his tail. "No, I'm afraid I can't do that. Olwin may have been an exceptional wizard, but he did a lousy job of preparing for his own death. You sit there like the old goat is worm bait." He dodged Talon's boot. "What did Olwin tell you about the Rite of Transference?" Talon looked blankly at the dragon. "I see. Ok, we've got a lot to cover. You'd better put a kettle on; this is going to take a while."

Graldiss and Talon sat by the fire late into the night. When Talon finally understood what was going to happen to him after sunrise the next day, he listened carefully to what his friend had to teach him. Many hours were spent reciting tongue-twisting Dragonese, memorizing complicated combinations of incantations and shifts of energy fields. By dawn Talon's mind was focused keenly on the ritual ahead.

The two friends stood at the opening of the cave, watching the lightening of the eastern sky. "Remember that you won't be alone today."

Talon nodded absently.

"They'll arrive soon. They won't be a pleasant lot, I'm sure. If you're lucky Keldric and Gildex will be unavoidably detained. The others will behave themselves."

Talon was paying little attention to the dragon's rambling. He wished the sun would move more quickly today. The sooner this was over the better.

The smooth rush of bodily relocation notified Talon that the spectators had arrived. He took a deep breath, slipped the Rings of Ko-Mon Po off his thumbs and put them into his pocket as Graldiss had instructed. He put on the blue silken robe and drew the hood over his head. He knew that Graldiss had taken care of the preparations in the meadow. He pulled in energy from the stone walls around him and relocated.

A large stone-slab table stood above the wildflowers. Talon stepped up slowly and placed his hands on the smooth surface. He did not look at those gathered before him. Five hooded figures moved to the table's edge. They stood motionless for a moment, waiting for the sun to keep its appointment.

At the instant when the sun appeared over the mountains giving color to the flowers around them, Talon pulled back his own hood. "I, Talon Morgale, call for the body of Olwin of Carthis."

Another wizard pushed back his hood. "I, Barkin Villiat, call for the body of Olwin the Wise."

"Oret the Mighty calls for Olwin to be brought forth." The old wizard sounded put out at this 'inconvenience'.

A melodic voice was next to call for Olwin's appearance. Talon guessed this was Fernley. "Olwin kind, Olwin great, grace us with your presence, let this boy receive his fate."

Poldrun was attired in a rich velvet robe, his cultured voice spoke firmly. "Most revered Olwin, we entreat you to appear before us."

The last one to call for Olwin's body was Keldric. "Don't keep us waiting, Old Fool." Talon noticed that Keldric wore a cap over his hair.

Talon pulled the hood back over his head, took a deep breath and silently entreated the stone table to give up its energy to him. He raised his hands to the brightening sky, silently chanted a practiced incantation then spoke in a loud voice. "Elint grrang linn rranta," he intoned the practiced words perfectly. He paid no attention to the outraged protests from Keldric and Oret, but noticed that Barkin put out a hand to restrain Keldric.

A shrouded body slowly materialized on the slab. Talon moved to Olwin's head. He placed his hands gently on the cold forehead. The others moved around the table and laid hands upon the body. "Crren nillya ssik rroon jall fa." Energy surged from the body below Talon's hands.

Olwin's spirit separated from the shrouded form and hung mistily above it. In their minds they all heard his words: "Welcome brothers. We have had our good times and bad times and now, you will finally be rid of me. As is my right on this occasion, I have gifts for each of you. Barkin, honor me by adding my small library to your own. Oret, you have always wanted a cave to call your own, please accept mine. Poldrun, I have held in secret, for these many centuries, the Sword of Timmian." Poldrun drew in a sharp breath of excitement. "I'm sure you can find a worthy recipient for it. Keldric, in remembrance of your concern for my health, I give you my stock of healing herbs, potions, poultices, and remedies. Since

Gildex could not make it today, I'm sure he wouldn't mind receiving a few of my cats. Fernley, I have an ancient lute you may find some use for.

"And now, on to the business at hand. Let there be no doubt as to this boy's right to succeed me and inherit my power. As you see, he is more than meets the eye and will soon surprise you all. Talon, young warrior, you have surpassed my highest expectations of you. Don't fear what is to come, embrace your destiny. Know that I will always be with you." The misty form condensed into a tight beam of light and shot into Talon.

Talon was prepared for the energy that burst within his mind. Graldiss had drilled into him how to keep a tight rein on the riot of thoughts and emotions that could engulf him. He raised his hands, palms down, over the empty husk of his mentor. "Torr blonn linn krra!" The shroud collapsed, no longer supported by a corpse, and within moments even the shroud disintegrated into dust and blew away in the breeze. "Billian taa." Talon said weakly slumping against the stone slab. The exertion of the Ritual had been tremendous.

Fernley was the first to reach Talon. "Very impressive, young man. Where did you learn to speak Dragon?"

"This was an outrage!" Oret's face was twisted in revulsion. "You insult us by uttering that disgusting language."

Talon knew he had made an enemy of Oret, but Keldric was the one he was more concerned about. Keldric hated dragons beyond reason. He saw Barkin wasn't close enough now to hold Keldric back. Hatred shown unguarded in his eyes, he took a menacing step toward Talon. Keldric pulled in energy from the ground. Within seconds he was at his full strength. He raised his arm, pointing to Talon. Just as he began to utter a complex spell a cat-sized dragon landed on the outstretched arm. Keldric screamed and fell backwards, expelled energy flashed around him, burning the grass and flowers.

Graldiss flew to the stone table. "Wizards!" he said with disgust. He turned to Talon, "Nicely done. But you're not finished, yet." He looked up, the wizards followed his gaze.

Hundreds of dark specks were flowing across the sky, toward the meadow. The specks grew larger: to the size of insects, then birds, and there soon was no doubt as to the identity of the swooping forms. The sky over the meadow darkened, a riotous wind from hundreds of colorful wings blew dust and leaves into the air. The frightened wizards turned to run, but found themselves held magically, forced to be witnesses. Dwarfed by the magnificent beasts, Spring trotted happily in the meadow.

Talon stared as the multitude of dragons landed with precision. Some distant part of his mind complained that the flowers would all be crushed. He looked to Graldiss for an answer.

"Another waits for you," his friend said simply. "Call for her."

Talon was too muddled to understand. Olwin's essence gave Talon a mental kick. *Don't be dense! Look at them. This is amazing. The old lady gave no hint.* Realization dawned on Talon and his knees weakened. This was more than he had bargained for. And he wasn't being given a choice. *Don't complain, just do it!*

Talon took a deep breath. "I, Talon, The Chosen One, call for the body of Magrid, Queen of Dragons!"

Graldiss perched on the edge of the stone slab. "I, Graldiss, The Reduced, beg the Great Matriarch to enter our presence." Talon noted that his friend had joined him in the reference to the Dragon Prophecy.

Three immense dragons walked up to the stone slab. In Dragonese they called for their Queen.

Talon raised his hands to the sky. "Elint grrang linn rranta," he said softly. The importance of the event lay heavily on his mind. Graldiss' tail whipped at Talon. With more enthusiasm he recited again: "Elint grrang linn rranta!"

A golden shroud materialized on the stone, the huge form of a dragon easily discernable beneath. Talon moved to the end of the table and placed his hands on the massive head. Graldiss and the other dragons spread their wings over the body of their

Queen. Talon felt an odd unity with these magnificent beasts. With pride he called forth Magrid's spirit: "Crren nillya ssik rroon jall fa!"

The air around them became electric. Lightning flashed in the clear sky followed by rolling thunder, colored sparks swirled in every direction. Above their heads, the magnificent orange form of the dragon matriarch appeared. A soft and gentle voice filled Talon's mind: "Greetings children." The look on the faces around him, told Talon that every creature in the meadow heard the words. "I am pleased that you have carried out my final wish. Before you stands a boy, born of magic, the Krrig Daa, the Chosen One, who will bring peace between our two races. As my heir, he is worthy of all the respect you would show me. Talon, the road ahead will not be easy, but the most crucial paths rarely are. You did not ask for what I am about to give you, but please accept this gift and the love with which it is given. The power I impart unto you will aid you in the task before you."

Talon braced himself for the rush of energy as he had felt when he accepted Olwin's power. He was uncertain he would be able to handle Magrid's power which he knew would be much stronger than Olwin's. A shaft of the purest light shown down on Talon. The energy that poured into Talon was not a fierce bolt, but a warm glow that filled his mind and soul. He raised his hands over the golden shroud. "Torr blonn linn krra!" The body that had been the

Queen vanished; golden flowers sprouted from the stone. In one voice Talon and the multitude of dragons cheered with jubilation: "Billian taa!" Talon fell to his knees. "It is done."

The dragons standing around the stone bowed low to Talon, and then flew off. The other dragons rose from the meadow in unison, bowed their heads and flew away. The spell holding the wizards was released. Oret spat on the ground and disappeared. Fernley sat heavily on the ground, a look of wonder on his face. He pulled out a pad of paper from his cloak and began scribbling. Barkin and Poldrun went to Talon's side.

No one was watching Keldric. The appearance of his wizard's staff was not noticed. The intake of energy went unobserved. The quietly muttered spell drew no attention. This would be his only chance since Talon did not have on the Rings that could protect him. With determined swiftness Keldric moved around the stone table. The staff was brought down with pinpoint accuracy. The spell's release trigger was savagely spoken. Keldric stood back gloatingly to watch the results.

They were not the results he expected. Talon was not writhing on the ground in agony; there were no flames, no melting flesh, no shattering of bone. Talon stood before him, unharmed. The energy released by Keldric's spell swirled around Talon's head, making his hair stand on end. With a deep, easy breath,

Talon drew in the energy. A faint suggestion was made from a new corner of his mind. "Be gone," he said softly.

Keldric stood stiffly, waiting for the power to strike. He was not relocated as he assumed he would be. Talon's words seemed to have no effect on him at all. He grinned menacingly. "All that power in a useless vessel," he scoffed. "Can't even move me an inch." He raised his staff and spoke the words that would send Talon to a frequently-used snake pit.

An unmoved Talon stood calmly before Keldric. "You misunderstood the meaning of my words."

Keldric's eyes opened wide in horror. He nervously uttered the simplest of spells, calling a stone to his hand. The stone remained mockingly next to his foot. He began screaming spells until he was out of breath. Madness filled his eyes, in desperation he reached out for Talon's serene face.

Graldiss quickly flew to protect his friend. Keldric grabbed the interfering dragon around the neck and squeezed tightly. "This is all *your* doing," he shrieked insanely. The small dragon flailed helplessly, scratching viciously, with no effect.

Talon began to understand what Magrid's power made him capable of doing. He directed his own energy to his friend. "Grow!"

Keldric didn't comprehend what was happening and continued his stranglehold while Graldiss' neck grew to the size of a tree trunk. When Keldric found himself being lifted off his feet he relinquished his hold. He fell to the ground weeping. Talon, feeling pity for the broken man, relocated him to a quiet field outside the village.

Barkin and Poldrun stared at Talon, fear mixing with admiration at the amazing power the young man now wielded. Graldiss was checking himself out, making sure he was in proper working order. Talon now felt energized. He threw back the hood of his robe, his white hair blowing in the breeze. "Wow, that was something. Anyone know how I did that?"

"Well, after what we saw today, I wouldn't be surprised at anything you did." Fernley, the only one not awed, stood and took Talon by the arm. "What do you say we go to a more comfortable location?" They all moved to Olwin's cave. From inside his robe Fernley brought out a flask and passed it to Barkin. He consulted the scroll he had been scribbling on earlier. "Did the Matriarch say that you were 'born of magic'?"

Talon looked self-conscious. "Apparently I was born with the ability to use magic. Olwin and Magrid both thought it was important."

Poldrun took a long drink from Fernley's flask. "You're joking, right? No one has ever been *born* with the power. Sure, there have been stories, but no real proof that it could happen."

Barkin finally stopped staring at Talon as if he were one of his specimens. "So that's why Olwin wanted to go through my library. He was looking for some confirmation. What about this business about being the Chosen One?"

Talon sat by the fire. "Well, there seems to be some prophecy—"

"Yes, of course!" Fernley dug through his inside pockets, tossing books and scrolls out onto the table. "There was a ballad from the Crinnelian mountain folk...here it is, they sang a lot about dragons, ballads of valorous knights, lullabies of dragonsong, battle hymns, childhood rhymes—"

"Get on with it," Poldrun interrupted gruffly.

"Yes, well there was one ballad which mentions... here I'll read it: 'The Beasts of the Wing have fled, our skies no longer glitter with their color, the wind carries not their song, their magic has left the land. Weep, children, for our loss. Watch for the day of their return. Keep vigil for the mage-born who will mend the wound. Rejoice when the Chosen calls them home.'" Fernley closed the book and looked pointedly at Talon. "Does that match up with what you were told?"

"Yes, close enough. Magrid told me that I had fulfilled their prophecy of the Krrig Daa that would bring dragons and humans together again, to end the war between our races. Olwin suspected something when he first hired me to retrieve the Rings. But I don't think he *really* knew until Magrid came to see me for herself."

Poldrun paced around the room. "That really doesn't matter now. What matters is that you have inherited the powers of a strong wizard and the dragon matriarch. That gives you more power than anyone alive."

"Poldrun's right," Barkin said grudgingly. "Those weren't simple tricks you did out there. If you aren't careful you could find yourself the puppet of some would-be emperor. And don't forget Keldric. He may be crazed at the moment and without power, but he'll soon come to his senses and when he does he'll come after you any way he can."

Talon wished that Graldiss were small enough to be there to counsel him. He called out to his friend's mind. "Are you still out there?"

"Of course. You don't think I'd leave now, do you? Thank you for putting me back to normal size. It'll take some getting used to, though." He chuckled at the irony.

Talon smiled at his friend's dilemma. "Just tell me which size you want to be and I'll arrange it. I don't suppose you've been listening to what's going on in here, have you?"

Talon could almost see Graldiss grin. "They're right, you know. You have more power than the world has seen for millennia. The choices you make in the next hour will shape the future of our world."

"What about Keldric? He could team up with Oret or Gildex and come looking for revenge."

Talon heard his friend laugh. "Didn't you notice all those big beasts in your front yard? You won't need to worry about protection ever again!"

Talon turned from the fire and looked at the three expectant faces. "I don't think I'll have to worry about Keldric, or anyone looking to use me as their pawn. Apparently I have made some pretty dedicated friends today. But you're right about the power I've inherited. I'm going to have to learn how to use it wisely."

Poldrun stood and put his hand on Talon's shoulder. "You will need an advisor." He felt, with his credentials, the choice was obvious.

Talon nodded, "You're right, of course." He stood and began to gather his personal belongings. "Do you think Oret will want to move in right away?" he asked light-heartedly. It didn't take him long to collect what he would need. In fact, everything fit into the worn pack Olwin had given him only a few months before. He looked around fondly. He opened Olwin's battered trunk and pulled out two silk wrapped packages. He unwrapped a gold and silver inlaid lute and handed it to Fernley. He handed the still wrapped sword to Poldrun, who clasped the mythical sword to his chest. "You'll find most of Olwin's books in the small cavern to the left," Talon told Barkin. "And there are some above his workbench."

Talon took one last look at the only place he could really call home. "Now it's time for me to leave."

Poldrun nodded and led the way out of the cave.

Talon stood next to Graldiss. "I know you expected me to take Poldrun as my advisor, but my destiny lies elsewhere. If I am going to repair the rift between man and dragon I will need to learn more about them. And who better to learn from than the dragons themselves." Talon climbed onto the back of his full-sized friend. Fernley grinned, knowing this was a proper ending to the epic he planned to write. Barkin could not fault Talon's logic and secretly wished he could join him. He always dreamed of studying dragon anatomy. Poldrun was chagrined to lose his chance to be the advisor to the most powerful man alive.

"It will probably take me centuries to learn how to wield this new power properly. I won't be making any quick decisions about how to fulfill this prophecy. And I'll be sure to consult you all before I do anything hasty."

Graldiss rose high into the air, where two massive red dragons met him. They flew north, toward the Crinnelian Mountains. "I hope you remembered your flute."

## Chapter 10

Talon shifted uncomfortably on the back of the greenish-brown dragon. It had been hours since he had mounted his reptilian friend, and the lack of padding on the scaled back was making the ride unbearable. He had used magic earlier to numb his rear and protect him from the freezing winds. But there was only so much that magic could do. Talon was very relieved to see the craggy peaks on the Crinnelian Mountains, their final destination.

Talon asked Graldiss about the ballad the Fernley had read. Graldiss explained that Magrid had only recently moved the colony back to the caverns within the Crinnelian Mountains. She must have felt the prophecy was upon us.

Squinting his eyes against the cutting wind, Talon looked down on the scene passing far below with his new multiple perspectives. As a battle strategist he saw the land below as strategically advantageous, the mind of the old wizard was concerned with the distance he would fall if Graldiss were to encounter turbulence, and Magrid's thoughts were flashes of favorite hunting spots. Talon knew he would have to meld the various thoughts in his mind if he was going to stay sane.

The escorting dragons began to angle downward. Talon did not see the entrance to the caverns until they were within a few feet. He was amazed at the agility of the dragons as he watched each one swoop into the small opening. The closeness of the entrance was deceiving and there was more than enough room for the dragons to wait just inside the rough opening. Graldiss walked to the front of the group and bent down to allow Talon to dismount.

Talon followed quickly behind Graldiss as they moved through the tunnels. He quickly became lost in the multitude of twists and turns. As they moved deeper into the mountain Talon noticed the walls of the tunnel glowed slightly. Magrid's memory explained that a special moss grew on the walls reacted to magic with a light yellow glow. The tunnel opened suddenly onto a large cavern. The glow of the walls was almost blinding. After a few moments Talon saw hundreds of dragons filling the cavern floor and lining a wide shelf half-way up the cavern wall. The cavern was oddly silent for the number of bodies within.

Graldiss led Talon to a platform at the cavern's center. A gray dragon, who still stood head and shoulders above Talon, waited on the dais. Talon found the name of Tollina pushed into his thoughts. Graldiss stepped aside and Talon walked the remaining distance by himself. As he climbed the high steps to stand next to the gray dragon a humming began on the shelf and moved to the cave floor. When he reached the top step, the humming grew into a roar. Tollina opened wide his wings and the cave went silent.

Tollina turned to Talon and looked deep into his eyes. Talon felt the dragon's mind push gently against his, he relaxed and allowed the dragon to read his thoughts. Tollina seemed to be searching for something and grinned widely when she found what she was looking for and withdrew from Talon's mind. She tilted his head back and let out a high-pitched cry. It was echoed by the multitude. Talon was soon overwhelmed by the hundreds of dragons surging toward him.

Talon was grateful to Tollina for ending the festivities before he fainted. He must have been introduced to two hundred dragons and the last seventy-five were a blur of color and fangs. Each one was allowed to look into his mind; to witness that he had truly been given the Matriarch's essence and to see that Talon's intentions were pure. Talon's head had begun to feel like a bowl of gruel being checked for maggots. But he smiled through it all, or at least grinned amiably.

Graldiss had already begun to transport the hundreds of gifts that had been brought. Talon had stopped counting the nuggets of gold and rough gems that were laid at his feet. He longed to look more closely at the bone and ivory statues nestled amongst the shining treasure.

"There will be a meeting of the Council of Elders tomorrow." Graldiss mentioned as he sent a stack of furs to Talon's cavern. "They have asked you to be available if they choose to speak with you."

After the reception he had just received, Talon thought the comment was a curious one. His ego was still bloated. "Do they want me to just wait around for them?" he asked.

Graldiss scowled at Talon. "These are important dragons, not the lot that came here tonight. These are the regents for the future queen. They were chosen for their wisdom and even-mindedness. You will not be easily accepted by them, so walk carefully."

"Are you telling me they won't accept that I carry Magrid's essence?"

"They may think you have taken it by force, or trickery. You are a wizard after all, and they don't trust wizards." The last of the gifts were sent away. "Just try to watch your step, and be humble."

Talon laughed at his friend's serious tone. "When have you ever known me to be anything *but* humble?" He disappeared, relocating himself to his new home.

The elders did indeed call on Talon the next day. They kept him waiting outside the meeting cave for some time before having him brought before them. Talon expected them to look into his mind as the others had done the night before, but none of the large dragons approached him.

"Thank you for coming to this meeting," Tollina said in greeting. "The members of the council would like to have a few words with you."

"More than a few, Tollina." A gray dragon with squinty eyes glared at Tollina for a moment then turned her attention to Talon. "We have brought you here to determine your place in our society." Her words did not sound welcoming as Tollina's had.

"What Manett means to say," a friendly green dragon added, "is that we are uncertain what role you, as the Krrig Daa, will take with our colony."

"No, Pettik, that is *not* what I meant." Manett interrupted. "A human has no place with dragonkind. I find it highly suspicious that our greatest matriarch would choose a human to give her power to. Some of us are not easily persuaded that you are the fulfillment of prophecy."

Talon nodded. "I fully understand your apprehension. I would be suspicious were the circumstances reversed."

Manett was not impressed with Talon's candor. "Well then why don't you tell us what your plans are for your life among the enemy?"

Talon did not take the bait. "I really have no plans. I've had little time to adjust. Magrid told me a few months ago that I was the Chosen One, which I still find hard to understand, but she did not tell me what she had in mind after her death. I was as shocked as anyone. But who am I to deny the decision of the Matriarch?"

"And how could you resist the advantages?" Manett said so softly that only Talon heard. "What part do you intend to take in our colony?"

Talon knew an adversary when he saw one. Nothing he could say would satisfy Manett, so Talon aimed his answer at the other elders. "Even with Magrid's memories I have a lot to learn. I don't think she meant for me to fulfill the prophecy immediately. I don't know what role you would like me to take, but I'm open to suggestions."

Manett's jaw tightened but she made no comment. Tollina was pleased with Talon's answer. "I have already confirmed the presence of the Matriarch's spirit. Does anyone dispute this?" Three wings lifted.

Talon tried not to feel offended by their doubt. He stepped up and waited while two dragons laid their front foot on his head and sifted through his thoughts to find what they were looking for. He was glad their touch was lighter than the dragons he had opened up to the night before.

The third dragon, Manett stood menacingly before Talon. She was repulsed by the thought of having to touch a human and looking into its mind was repugnant. But she wouldn't take anyone else's word on the matter. She stretched her arm out and placed one claw on the white hair. She took a deep breath and looked into Talon's mind.

Talon put all of his private thoughts behind a mental barrier and steeled himself for the nasty thoughts that were about to invade his own. He was surprised to find fear behind Manett's hate. He cleared a path to Magrid's essence. The sooner Manett found it the sooner she'd be out of his head.

Manett did not care to waste any time spying on the human's thoughts. She supposed she ought to be grateful that he left so few of them lying around for her to wade through. She was drawn to a secluded corner of the human's mind.

"Was my choice *so* terrible?" that which was once Magrid asked.

"Yes!" Manett pulled her thoughts away and tried to escape. In her haste she bumped into another pocket of unopened essence.

"Hey, watch out. Can't a dead guy get some rest around here?"

Manett pulled away as if she were burned. This was a wizard's power! She had not known that this human was more than just a freak of magic holding hostage to the Matriarch's energy. But if he held the unreleased power of a wizard, then this human was doubly dangerous. She fled, careful not to bump into anything else.

When Manett was free of Talon's mind, she glared at him, then turned to the waiting council members. "What ever decision you make about this human leave me out of it. I do not, nor ever will, trust any human." She stomped out of the cave.

Tollina was disappointed, but not surprised at Manett's reaction. She looked at the rest of the council, then at Talon. "We welcome you into our colony. Your place among us will show itself with time. Your companion Graldiss will be your guide." The other council members nodded agreement, and Talon knew he was dismissed.

Out in the tunnel Talon considered what had just happened. Apparently he was accepted by the elders, with the exception of Manett, but was given no real place in the colony. It didn't really matter to Talon, Magrid hadn't given him any idea what being the Krrig Daa was all about, so he was going to have to improvise until he figured out what he was supposed to do.

The next day Graldiss took Talon on a tour of the tunnels and caves. Talon hoped that he wouldn't be expected to know his way around right away. Later, in his own cave, there were plenty of visitors. Some were just curious; others hoped to see their Chosen One do something special. When the last dragon left, Talon dropped exhausted into his bed and promptly fell asleep.

Talon woke in the dark. Without thinking he made a ball of yellow light. The light hung in the air for a few moments before drifting down to settle on the ground. Sleepily, Talon realized that he was not in his cavern in Olwin's cave. Memories began to seep in and he rolled off of the soft bed. His new home was an empty side-cavern at the end of a maze of tunnels. Graldiss had arranged that a fur-stacked bed be brought in for him and an over stuffed chair was placed next to the fire alcove. A work table with shelves was covered with the precious gems and intricate carvings that had been given to him. It was deeper and more isolated than his old home had been and Talon knew it would take a few days to get used to the idea of living deep within a mountain. But, it was a roof over his head, so he shouldn't complain. After giving Olwin's cave to Oret, Talon was glad he didn't have to sleep out in the open.

Talon lay quietly on his soft bed and listened. He slowly tuned out the sounds around him, soft silver-toned singing, a muffled argument, the whistle of the wind, the hum of the glowing moss. Talon then focused on the sounds within his own body. Blood and muscles were calmed, thoughts stilled.

Deep in Talon's mind was a stirring. A quiet conversation was taking place. Talon listened carefully.

"What *more* will he need, they accepted him."

"They were not all there. He has a good head start, and that will take him far. We will need to begin his training."

"So soon? Can't we give him a few days to acclimatize?" The voice was old and tired.

The soft chuckle had a massive feel to it. "Will his enemies wait while he acclimatizes? Do *you* want to wait?"

Talon knew the question was aimed at *him*. "Better to take steps to avert an attack than to face it directly." He turned his vision inward. "Can I see you?"

The old man laughed. "What would you have us appear in? You spoke the words that dissipated our physical bodies."

"Don't tease the boy. Picture a setting," Magrid's voice explained, "where we can talk, and ease your mind into it."

Talon thought a moment. Graldiss had warned him against altering his appearance, would this be the same thing? Once he changed his mental vision, would he be stuck with it?

"It's just a mind game; no real change will take place. You aren't really *hearing* us; it's just your way of dealing with the perception of our thoughts."

Talon thought of the meadow outside Olwin's cave. He envisioned Olwin and Magrid as he saw them before they died. He placed his own body in the scene rather than outside looking in. He was not prepared for the joy he felt at seeing his mentor.

"And there lies the danger of this type of communication." Olwin looked serious. "The temptation to stay is hard to resist."

Magrid nodded. "It is best if this is the only time we talk like this." She looked down at herself, turning to see the gleaming orange scales. "The temptation is not all yours, either. This is like a chance for us to be *alive* again."

Olwin scowled and began pacing. "Let's say what needs to be said."

Talon felt tears slide down his cheeks. He didn't want to lose them again. He put his hand up. Were these *real* tears?

"As real as you make them." Olwin's tone softened. "Don't let your emotions run amok."

Talon got a hold of himself. "Tell me what I need to know." His imagination sat cross-legged in the flowers; with a tweak he included their scent.

Magrid took a deep breath. "You already know that your power has changed."

Talon nodded. "What I did to Keldric and Graldiss."

"Yes, but there is much more."

Olwin interrupted. "In fact, there is little that you *can't* do, now."

"A dragon's power is far greater than has ever been let on." Magrid revealed. "Even the youngest of us can outstrip a full-fledged wizard." Olwin stared at the Matriarch. She laughed at his expression. "Do you really think we gave you as much power as *we* had? That's a bit egotistical. No, we taught you what you needed to know to advance your race, and that's all. But it was also decided to hide this superior power from our own kind, as well. We knew there were dragons that would destroy your race if they knew they could, just as you tried to destroy us."

"But we tried to destroy you. How could you let that happen?"

"It was not an easy thing to watch thousands die. But if the truth had come out I could not have controlled them and it would have been genocide. I had to believe that the prophecy was true, and we would survive."

Talon hoped he could be as brave as Magrid when faced with similar circumstances. "Who else knows this?" Talon felt both thrilled and afraid of this new information.

"Only you and the new Queen. Our whole history is passed down through the queens, but this knowledge is held only by my line. Not even the other queens suspect this. That is one reason I made sure of your...goodness." Magrid paused. "I'm sorry, but you will not be allowed to pass on your power and knowledge to an apprentice."

Talon saw the logic to this, and accepted the judgment. "We need to make sure I never fall into the hands of a dark wizard. I'll let Graldiss know that I'm to be sacrificed if necessary." Talon was amazed at the matter-of-factness of his own voice.

"You will need to be careful when you use this extreme power. Better to be discreet about using magic."

Olwin agreed. "Your exhibition yesterday is enough to give anyone second thoughts about challenging you."

Talon cocked his head, a thought just occurred to him. "How long will you two be in my head? Will I be able to confer with you when things get sticky?"

Magrid smiled. "How long did you want me to be stuck with this old man? We have two days until our individual personalities must leave you. Our memories are yours now, and when we are gone you will have to dredge through them for any answers you need."

"So I suggest you take advantage of us while we're still here."

Secretly Talon was glad he would not have these two arguing inside his head for the next two hundred years. "We'd better get started, then, don't you think?"

Magrid stood and shook out her small wings. "I like this boy," she said to Olwin.

"Sure, but he's going to make us work on an empty stomach." Olwin slouched lower against a tree stump.

Graldiss looked in on Talon many times over the next two days. He understood the after-effects of the Rite of Transference in theory, but had never actually seen it take place. He kept everyone out of the cave, saying that The Chosen One needed time to meditate. Talon mumbled words from time to time, even shouted out in Dragonese, but he made little sense. Graldiss brought food and water, Talon would need it after the ordeal.

When Talon stepped out of the depths of his mind he cried for the first time in his life. When he emptied himself of grief, Talon devoured the chicken and fruit laid out on the table and sat in front of the lit fire pit. His body and mind were worn out. The military training he had gone through was nothing compared to what he had just experienced.

Graldiss noticed a change in his friend. There was a depth of maturity that was a bit unnerving. It was odd when Talon played an old hunting song that Graldiss had been taught as a youngling. He found that Talon no longer needed a guide in the tunnels. Graldiss missed his position as escort. He had to admit, though, that he enjoyed conversing with

Talon in Dragonese. Talon was now fluent, but he had a definite accent.

Talon had a difficult few weeks of getting used to his new dragon perspective. With Magrid's knowledge he now saw dragons in a new light. Their scale patterns and horn twists were handed down from their mothers, their voice patterns from their fathers. Talon soon began to pick out family lines. He began to see the innate magic the dragons used every moment of their lives. The music created by that magic, ringing within the tunnel walls, became more distinct; complex melodies, repeating rhythms, and discordant harmonies.

Talon was eager to see Magrid's egg that held Ittra, the new Queen. The egg sat in a place of honor in the hatching cavern. Tollina saw no harm in allowing the Krrig Daa to visit the Queen egg, but Manett objected strongly, only bowing to the rest of the council when she saw that this was not a fight she was going to win.

Graldiss did not accompany Talon to visit the Queen. He did not feel worthy of the privilege. Tollina came to take Talon to the massive hatching cavern. Manett insisted on being present as well.

Talon expected the cavern where all the dragons laid their eggs to be hot, but it wasn't until he stepped onto the cool sands that Magrid's memory came to mind, and Talon knew that the internal temperatures of a dragon egg could get extremely high and the cool sands and circulating outside air kept them from overheating. He admired the clusters of blue, red and green eggs. If he stared at the shells long enough he saw the colors swirl in strange patterns. Talon heard low mumbling in his mind coming from one of the older clutches. He recalled that the unhatched dragons talked to each other. No wonder clutchmates were so close. Talon found himself standing before the Queen egg. The brilliantly white egg visibly swirled with eddies of gold. Without straining, Talon could hear singing coming from inside the shell.

Tollina leaned down and whispered to the egg. Talon's heart sang with the clear pure laughter that came from the egg. Manett stiffened and scowled. Tollina motioned for Talon to come closer. He hesitated, but could not resist the pull of the beautiful shell. As he neared the sandy nest, Talon reached out his hand. Manett objected, but he was silenced by the Queen. When Talon's hand touched the warm shell his heart leapt and he cried out with joy.

"Hello Krrig Daa. I am glad to finally meet you."

Talon fell to his knees. The voice in his mind was that of a young child, but the thoughts that touched his were ancient. He didn't feel worthy of being in her presence.

The Queen laughed again. "Silly, if not you, then who else could be worthy?"

Talon sat cross-legged next to the egg. Tollina politely retreated, dragging Manett with her. Talon gently touched the egg, pulling back slightly when his emotions got too strong. When he felt in control of himself he spoke softly, "Greetings Queen Ittra, Magrid sends her love."

Flashes of warm memories came from the Queen. "May I touch her mind?"

Talon wanted to accept the honor the Queen was requesting of him, but he didn't think he could survive the deep mental connection such a thing would take.

Ittra sensed Talon's hesitation. "Perhaps another time." There was a feeling of curiosity. "Krrig Daa, your mind is strange, not like the others that come to see me."

Talon smiled, the Queen could see into his mind, but she could not see him. "I am a man."

The flash of revulsion crushed Talon, but it was quickly replaced by a burst of laughter. "That's very funny. That must have come as quite a shock to the others."

"Yes, it did. I'm still having a hard time accepting it myself." Talon told Ittra of the morning Magrid broke the news of the dragon prophecy to him. "It was not at all what I had planned for my life."

"We must follow the path destiny lays before us." Ittra spoke of her own destiny as much as of Talon's.

Talon wondered if Ittra was thinking of the great secret she and Talon were charged to keep.

"We all have secrets," Ittra said, reading Talon's thoughts. "Ours is just a bit bigger than most. She paused, something bothered her. "There is something else about you that is different." Talon felt her trying to remember something. A shout of surprise was audible from inside the egg. "You are a wizard! Oh, this is too funny!"

It was some minutes before Talon decided to interrupt the giggles. "There are some that don't see the humor in this situation."

"I bet not. Manett for one. I wondered why she was so sour lately." Again Ittra fell deep into thought. "A wizard; that must be how the prophecy of the earth giving her power to the Krrig Daa was fulfilled."

"Actually, that provision was satisfied before I gained Olwin's power. I was told that I was somehow born with the knowledge of magic."

Ittra was impressed. "That makes you more special than any human in your history." The Queen breathed deeply. "I am tired. Will you promise to come back and visit with me tomorrow?"

Talon gently rubbed the smooth shell. "Of course, your majesty."

"And bring your Graldiss with you. He should be proud of the part he played in bringing you to us." Her voice faded.

Talon rose shakily to his feet. He was near tears at the loss of the young Queen's presence in his mind. He met Graldiss in the passageway outside the hatching cavern and they returned to Talon's cave in silence.

When Talon thought he could trust his voice, he told Graldiss of his meeting with the Queen. "I don't think I've been so completely happy."

Graldiss nodded. "I've heard that her voice alone has made many fall in love with her."

"That would be an advantage for a queen. How long has she been...when did Magrid lay her?"

"A year ago. She became conscious about 5 months ago. It's uncertain when she will hatch; it can take many years for the Queen to understand everything she must know to rule well." Graldiss stretched out and let the flames warm his belly. "Will you be going back to talk to her again?"

Talon nodded, "Every day if they'll let me. Manett didn't like the idea at all, but Tollina seemed to accept it alright." His flute appeared in his hand. "She wants me to bring you next time I visit." Talon played a light tune and watched Graldiss blush. The dragon said nothing, but there was a silly grin on his face for the rest of the night.

Over the next weeks Talon visited Queen Ittra everyday. They spoke of humans and dragons. They discussed on plans to bring the two species together.

The spoke of the secret power they held and how they could use it to better the bond between man and dragon. Some days Graldiss would join Talon in the hatching cave, but he was uncomfortable speaking to the unhatched Queen. Ittra found this endearing and would tease Graldiss mercilessly. Talon felt these were the happiest days of his life.

Manett was not at all pleased at the attention Talon received from her Queen. Manett kept a close eye on Talon. Questioning his movements and frowning at the number of young dragons that followed him around. She often commented on the odor of human permeating the mountain since Talon had moved in.

Talon did not ignore the scrutiny of the elder dragon. He knew that he would have a hard time being accepted by the older dragons. Many of them had vivid memories of the vicious knights who hunted them to near-extinction. But most of them accepted the presence of Magrid's power and left the rest to destiny. Manett's hatred of humans was obvious and Talon knew not to be caught alone with her in a side tunnel.

By the time Talon had been in the mountain for a month he had a comfortable pattern set. Graldiss would join him for breakfast when they would talk about news from the caves and neighboring mountain colonies. Then Graldiss would go hunting or visit his clutchmates, Talon would visit other dragons or wizards and get a feel for how he could bring about this 'bridging of two species' he had been prophesied to do.

Talon didn't like prophesies. They tended to give the end results with no details of how to get there. He was smart enough to know that he was not going to be able to bring about change overnight. It would take years, maybe decades to break through the wall of hatred both sides had for the other. Any discussions Talon had with the dragon council about cooperation with humans usually arrived at the assumption that humans would be subservient to dragons. He found that most wizards felt exactly the opposite and looked forward to obtaining more of the dragons' magical abilities. Talon was glad his life expectancy had been lengthened; this might take a couple of centuries

Prophesies created another problem: fanatical followers. Talon had never liked mindless fanatics; he had run into quite a few in his profession as mercenary and had learned that they were more dangerous because they tended not to question their leaders. Talon preferred someone with brains who believed in his causes. But Talon also knew that he had to tread softly with these followers.

## Chapter 11

"*They're* here." Talon smiled at the sarcasm in Graldiss' voice.

"How many today?"

"Twenty, maybe twenty-five." Graldiss would have happily tossed them all down a cliff.

Talon sighed, more than yesterday. If their numbers grew by five every day there would soon be too many to handle. "Not enough room in here. Tell them I will meet them by the Stone Slab." Talon hadn't been back to the meadow since he had gained Olwin and Magrid's power and he wondered how he would feel being back.

Graldiss looked intently at Talon. "Are you sure that's a wise choice? You know they'll read some deep dark meaning to it."

Talon had to agree; they interpreted everything he did as sacred. He didn't want to think about what they did with his chamber pot. But he had a plan, and he needed to make a definite impression. "The slab, in twenty minutes." Talon wanted time to prepare.

Talon stood within the trees that circled the meadow where he was to speak to his *followers*. The wild flowers had yet to bloom around the large stone slab where Talon had performed the Rite of Transference only a few months earlier. For a moment he pictured the slab encircled by six wizards, each with hands outstretched over the shrouded figure of his mentor.

Talon had watched the dragons appear in the air above the meadow. They drifted down and formed a semi-circle around the stone. They evidently thought Talon was going to use the sacred stone as a pulpit to preach from. Talon waited for a few more minutes then relocated himself. He suddenly appeared, cross-legged, on the holy stone. A great hushed shock spread through those assembled. Talon had carefully chosen this attire for just the reaction he was now getting. His followers expected the Krrig Daa to wear a hooded wizard's robe, not an open-collared shirt and loose pants. They had grown used to seeing Talon's white hair curling wildly over his shoulders, and didn't know what to make of the close-cropped style he now wore. But what shocked the dragons most was Talon's irreverent position on their most honored artifact.

Before shock could turn into rebellion Talon began to speak. "Welcome friends. I am glad you could join me here this morning; here, where you and I are connected." His audience stilled. "As you know, today is the Feast of Korinot." Talon's followers looked at him blankly, he smiled and continued. "But rather than cutting off a piece of flesh to give to your neighbor, I would rather have you offer up some of your *wisdom*, so that we may all be enriched by each other's knowledge."

The dragons looked at each other, confused. They had never heard of the Feast of Korinot, and they certainly didn't want to eat each other. This was not what they had expected from their prophet. Nattrok, one of Talon's first disciples, stepped up to the stone. "I beg your forgiveness, Krrig Daa, but what wisdom can *we* give? You are the wisest of us, should you not speak so that we may learn?"

Talon wished his followers would not talk to him in that archaic way. "But don't you think you can learn from each other?" He turned to a newcomer, in hopes that their mind hadn't yet turned to mush. "Vanyett, what shape do you see the prophecy of the Krrig Daa taking in the coming years?"

The young dragon's mouth hung open. He stared at the prophet; the other dragons stared at him. Vanyett felt a wave of panic and tried to gather his thoughts.

"Come now," Talon coaxed, "you must have *some* thoughts on the matter." He turned to the waiting crowd. "If I am to accomplish the task before me I would like some advice of those around me. Would you rather I ask the Elders?"

Heads shook in unison. Vanyett took a deep breath and stepped forward. "To reach our final goal of unity between Dragonkind and humankind, we must first remove the wall both species have built."

Talon could have jumped for joy. Instead, he smiled broadly and nodded. "Yes, you have perfectly stated out first goal." Vanyett was congratulated by those around him. "Who has an idea what steps can be taken to achieve this goal?"

There was another long pause. Talon waited patiently. This time Nattrok stepped forward. "It is unlikely that humans would make the first move." He looked at Talon, mortified. "With the exception of you, Holy One."

Talon smiled. "Continue, please."

Nattrok swallowed the lump in his throat. "Other than you, Holy One, it is unlikely that any human would step forward and champion our cause. It then falls to dragons to take the first step."

"And that would be?"

Nattrok squinted his eyes in thought. "We must go out into the world of man and show them we are willing to be friends."

Talon nodded, this dragon's brain might not be mush after all. "Very good idea. Now why don't we discuss how such a task can be carried out?" He jumped off of the stone slab and walked among the dragons. He encouraged each one to give voice their ideas. The dragons began to listen to each other instead of him alone. Talon was thrilled. He might still be on a pedestal, but they had definitely stepped up a bit higher themselves. The only input he gave that morning was a human's perspective.

When Talon returned to the mountain he was anxious to tell Graldiss how the meeting went.

"Feast of Korinot? I've never heard of it. You made that up." Graldiss accused.

Talon laughed. "No, that's the funny part. I found it in Magrid's memories. It was a huge Winter's feast to pay tribute to the dragons that gave the ultimate sacrifice to keep their brothers alive. I just gave it a little twist."

The dragon shook his head. "Well, you may have convinced them to be a bit more independent, they are still followers, not leaders."

"That's where I thought you'd come in."

Graldiss stood for some moments in shock. "You've got to be kidding."

Talon hid his smile. "Why, don't you think *Little Brother* is worthy of such a task given to him by the most holy Krrig Daa?" Talon found himself landing heavily on his back, Graldiss' tail on his chest.

"Would the Chosen One like to push his luck?"

Talon transported himself across the cave and slammed a pillow across his friend's face. "Want to be the size of a cat again?"

A bag of flour emptied above Talon's head. Talon easily diverted it away toward Graldiss. Graldiss pushed back at the powder. The white cloud spun in the air between the two. Talon broke first, laughing so hard he fell to his knees. He sat back, covered with flour. "That one's yours," he coughed. The next minute the flour was gone. Talon lit the fire and moved a kettle over the flames. "You know, we've gotten way too serious lately."

Graldiss pushed a cushion near the fire pit. "Yeah, you've been acting like an old wizard. Lighten up. Whatever happened to the good old days?"

Talon plopped into his fireside chair. "Which days were those, before I met you and I killed soldiers for a living, or after I met you and I was tortured, kidnapped, and forced into an occupation I didn't want?"

"Whine, whine, whine. When are you ever going to grow up?"

Talon took the cup of tea Graldiss sent floating over to him. "From what I've seen, growing up isn't mandatory in this job. Besides, I'm only fifteen; I'd like to enjoy my youth before I have to be a mature adult."

Graldiss popped a cake into his mouth. "Don't give me that 'I'm only fifteen' line. You were never 'only fifteen', and now you've got a few centuries of memories floating around in your head. You were probably born mature. Besides, you are probably sixteen by now, so you can stop complaining." A piece of cake appeared in front of Graldiss. "Thanks. It just seems a bit boring around here."

"Why don't you get out for a while? You've been a great help to me but you don't have to baby-sit me." Talon tried to sound casual, but he really wasn't ready for his best friend to leave him.

Graldiss was quiet for some time. He did want to get out in the open again. Life in the mountain was a bit claustrophobic after being outside for so long. He felt a strong obligation to stay with Talon, but no one had said he couldn't take a break now and then. "You're right," he said after a while. "I think I'll go and roam around for a few days, check out the boars in Wittig Forest. They can get quite large, you know."

Talon thought about a dragon chasing an overgrown pig around a forest and smiled. "Bring me back the tusks."

Graldiss spent the rest of the evening with Talon, chatting and snacking. The next morning he snuck out before Talon woke. He deeply wished the wizard could come with him, but Talon was a bit of a celebrity now, and he couldn't just disappear for a week.

Talon found himself missing his friend more than he thought possible. The only other person he had been as close to in his life was Olwin, and it was hard to miss *him* since a piece of the old goat was still inside Talon's head. The mountain was oddly depleted of dragons. Many of Talon's followers were out searching for ways to assist humans, and the latest hatchlings had moved out to the canyon to practice flying and magic, but the tunnels seemed quieter than Talon had ever known them to be. He tapped Magrid's memories, but found nothing about migrations or evacuations.

Ittra had a more mundane reason for the lowered presence of her colony: hunting season. "They're all out getting fattened up," she explained. "You might want to put in a few provisions as well. Winters can be harsh up here, we get snowed in, firewood gets hard to find, fresh meat goes into hibernation."

Talon promised to go shopping before the first snow.

Before the week was out Talon deeply regretted urging Graldiss to take a vacation. Just after sunrise Talon was thrown out of bed by a tremendous jolt in the fabric of magic. He jumped to his feet and raced out of his cave. Talon slammed into Silgaa, one of Graldiss' clutchmates. "What's happened?" Talon asked, standing and catching his breath.

"A dragon is being killed!" Silgaa was out of breath and panicky

"Where? Here in the cave? Take me!" Talon didn't know what else to do.

Without asking, Silgaa transported both of them outside the mountain. "Get on. I don't know exactly where he's at, but I can fly in his direction."

Talon climbed onto Silgaa's rough shoulders and wrapped his arms tightly around the rough neck. With a jolting leap Silgaa thrust into the air and spread his wings. They flew off of the mountain range and toward the plain.

"Hurry! Can't we go faster?!" Talon knew he was being unfair to Silgaa but the urgency he felt was overwhelming.

Silgaa took a deep breath and beat his wings faster. "He's dying. We won't get there in time." Silgaa's thoughts were heavy.

Talon knew Silgaa was right. He could feel the exhaustion, the quiet release of the spirit. Tears of despair burned his eyes. When Silgaa cleared the trees Talon saw the distant fallen figures. He immediately transported himself to the dragon's side.

The ancient dragon was dead. His spirit drained into the ground as silently as its blood. A bent, rusted sword stuck obscenely from the once graceful neck. Talon looked vengefully around for the murderous knight.

"Over here." Silgaa landed heavily next to the dragon's head. A bloody hand held lifelessly to the reddened grass.

Talon turned the dragon over with care. A leather-clad knight lay crushed beneath the massive body. Legs and back were scorched. Talon couldn't tell whose blood stained the leather shirt.

"His name was Dissal." Silgaa's head rested gently on the fallen dragon. "He taught us flying tactics. He protected his whole clutch during an ambush. The Matriarch rewarded him with a ledge next to the fire pit. He was old, but flew out every morning to oversee the changing of the watch, and hunted with great precision." Talon heard a dangerous tone enter Silgaa's voice. "We would sit around the fire pit and listen to him tell stories all night."

Talon pulled off the knight's helmet. "It's an old man!" Silgaa looked over in astonishment. Thin white hair was matted down with sweat; old scars criss-crossed the wrinkled face. Something didn't feel right about this. Talon knelt down and laid his hands on the dampened grass. "May your roots run deep."

"May your feet be light." The many voices of grass chanted to Talon.

"You have suffered greatly in this battle."

"Yes, but we have also gained from its conclusion. The bravery of the knight strengthens our blades and the spirit of the majestic dragon will endure in our roots for generations."

"Will you tell me the story of this great battle?" Talon chose a nearby rock and sat down.

The blades of grass conferred with each other for a few minutes, then a single blade spoke to Talon. "Two great warriors met upon this field. They spoke cordially for a time. When the clouds hid the warm sun, the warriors took up battle postures. The mighty opponents traded blows; sword, scale, tail, shield. From time to time the two would cease their aggressions and rest. As the sun crossed the sky the warriors began to tire. They became careless. The dragon was the first to draw blood. The knight found a gap in the dragon's armored scales and thrust deeply. On and on they fought, each strike brought with it a heavy wound. In the end it was exhaustion that brought down the valiant warriors. The brave knight fell to the ground, his sword held upright only because it was wedged against a stone. The dragon leaned too heavily on his injured foreleg and fell forward. His weight drove the knight's sword deep into his own throat. As the mighty beast collapsed he fell onto the knight, killing him instantly. The dragon uttered an apology with his dying breath. And thus came the end of two valiant adversaries."

Talon wiped tears from his eyes, noticing Silgaa doing the same. "Adversaries, but not enemies. They must have known each other from previous battles and respected each other." Talon sent his thanks to the grass. "We are grateful for your story. Please take the energy that was spilled this day, and raise a memorial of wild flowers in their honor." Talon put his hand on Silgaa's shoulder. "Will you return to the caves and let the others know what's happened here.

Try to keep them from retaliating. This was a fight between friends."

Silgaa nodded. "I'll do my best."

Talon laid his hands on Dissal's body and began to focus his energy to allow the dragon's body to dissipate when he heard a cry of torment. In the distance he saw a dragon speeding toward him. When it was close enough, Talon saw it was a female of great age. Dissal's mate.

The dragon landed next to the body of her mate and surveyed the scene. She glared at Talon. "What happened? Why are you here?"

"I felt Dissal's death. I was unable to arrive in time to stop the fight. It was a fair and friendly fight that ended tragically. You can confirm that by talking to the grass."

The dragon did just that. After a few minutes, she sunk heavily to the ground. "The old fool." She began to sob.

Talon watched helplessly.

After a while the widowed dragon became quiet. "I should have known he would do something like this. He always said he would go down fighting." She kicked Dissal. "Idiot! What am I going to do without you?" She broke into tears again.

Talon started to go to the distraught dragon's side when he saw an old woman coming through the trees. Talon looked for some place to hide.

"Where is he?" The elderly woman looked from Talon to the dragon. "I know he's out here. His sword and armor are gone." She stopped and looked more closely at the scene before her. She squinted slightly and recognized the booted foot. She fell to the ground with an agonized wail. She pulled at the leg, pleading for Danya to get up. She looked to Talon. "Can you help him? I'm sure if you could just..." She began to sob again.

Talon stood silent. He breathed a calming spell and laid his hand on the old woman's shoulder.

The sun had begun to set before the tears of the two widows eased. The old woman wiped her eyes one last time and blew her nose. She stood and took a deep breath. She looked up at the dragon. "What have we done to deserve such daft old beasts?"

The elderly dragon nodded. "They grew stupid with age. What did they leave us with?"

"Debts and a leaky roof," the woman complained.

"A cold cave, and not enough wood to last the winter," the dragon added.

"Wood! Danya was supposed to go into town tomorrow and bring back a wagonload of wood. And who's going to butcher the hogs?" The old woman was quickly working herself into a state.

The ancient dragon was becoming just as angry. "Did he expect me to hunt at my age?"

Talon stared at the two widows. He almost laughed, these two should have been mortal enemies, and they were talking about hogs and wood. In a flash of inspiration, Talon saw an opportunity. "You both seem to have a lot in common."

The old lady turned to look at Talon. "I don't know who you are, boy, but I think you're a little presumptuous."

"I was just thinking this terrible event has placed the two of you in similar circumstances."

The old dragon stepped around her fallen mate and bowed. "Krrig Daa, you need not concern yourself with us. You must have more important things on your mind."

"Krrig-whatever-your-name-is I don't see how this matter is any of your business."

The widowed dragon shot a scolding look at the old lady, "Hold your tongue hag, this is a very holy man, and a powerful wizard."

"He didn't do much for my Danya," the woman said petulantly.

Talon scowled at the dragon's harsh words. "My name is Talon." He bowed to the old woman. "I can only say I'm sorry I arrived too late."

The old woman accepted his apology. She curtsied. "I am Loris." She looked down at her husband. "If it hadn't happened today, it would have been another day. Danya was forever picking fights. He's felt a bit sorry for himself since he was released from the Baron's army."

The dragon bowed again to Talon. "I am Kaalla. Dissal also was itching for a fight. The two of them may have been planning this for some time." She wiped a fresh tear from her eye and turned to Loris. "We were privileged to have two brave mates. And now we are alone."

Loris nodded. "They could have at least waited until spring."

Talon looked at the two widows. "There is a simple answer to both of your problems." The two turned their attention to Talon. "Why don't the two of you live together?" Both widows laughed. Talon did not. "I'm serious."

Loris covered her smile with her hand. "I know, that makes it even more amusing. We're a bit old to become roommates, don't you think? And I don't have room in my little cottage for a dragon."

Kaalla added, "She's a bit frail to be moving in to a cave."

Loris glared at the dragon. "Who are you calling frail? I'm not on my deathbed. You were the one complaining about a cold cave."

"Yes, I think it's the perfect solution." Talon said with finality. "Companionship and security, that's what you both need."

"But our mates just killed each other." Kaalla pointed out. "That doesn't make the best foundation for a friendship."

Loris was thinking of the pitying looks she would be getting the next time she went in to town. With Danya gone there would be vultures looking to take her land from her. This beast seemed a decent sort; she might be good company on long winter nights. "People and dragons don't get along." Loris said, but there was little conviction in her voice.

"That's only because they've never tried." Talon persisted.

"It would never be accepted, by either side." Kaalla reasoned, but she was beginning to warm to the idea. Widowed female dragons were expected to help raise the new hatchlings, and Kaalla didn't have the temperament for that. Besides, the woman seemed to have a lot of backbone. She was standing here arguing with a dragon, after all.

Talon saw that he would get no more arguments from the widows.

In the distance Talon could see five dragons flying toward them. Talon thought it best to send Loris on her way. "I think it best if you return home now Loris, this might get unpleasant."

Loris didn't like this youngster giving her orders, but if he was as powerful as the dragon thought he was, it might be wise to leave these matters to him. She looked up at Kaalla. "I look forward to meeting you again. I will light candles and pray for your mate tonight."

Kaalla lowered her head level with the woman's. "We will certainly be the topic of gossip. I will sing of the brave battle of our two mighty warriors."

Talon sent Loris off and prepared for the conflict that flew toward him. Kaalla turned to Talon. "Leave this to me. It is my right to claim or not claim vengeance for Dissal's death. They will not dispute my decision."

Talon was surprised to find Kaalla's words to be true. Even Manett would not argue against the widow's choice not to burn down the village that spawned the murderer of such a noble dragon as Dissal. Manett was suspicious of Talon's role in the matter. Four of the dragons carried the lifeless body back to the mountain, Kaalla flew sedately behind, and Silgaa carried Talon.

Over the next days Talon hired builders from the nearby village and oversaw the building of an extension to Loris' cottage. Talon's fanatical followers saw this as an ideal opportunity to work along side humans. Of course the villagers didn't quite see it the same way. Their basic distrust of the large monsters took a while to overcome. The builders immediately saw the advantage of such large beasts in moving large timbers and started making arrangements for the new assistants to work on other jobs.

The presence of a wizard and a pack of dragons kept sympathetic but greedy mourners to a minimum. Kaalla made short work of anyone stupid enough to suggest that her new roommate needed 'comfort in these dark days'. These mourners generally needed comforting themselves after Kaalla relocated them to the hog pen or compost heap. She didn't make many friends that day, but she felt it would be wise to be upfront with such people. Loris didn't seem to mind the strong-arm tactics of her new companion.

Two weeks after the strange project began the finishing touches were added and a team of dragons helped Kaalla move her belongings to her new home. Talon was feeling very pleased with himself. This might be a small step in improving human-dragon relations, but at least it was a step in the right direction. Loris didn't care about Talon's lofty plans; she just wanted everyone out of her house so she could get things back to normal. Kaalla agreed and shooed everyone off at the earliest opportunity.

Many of Talon's followers saw advantages to live-in integration and asked their Krrig Daa to find them similar situations. Talon first approached Poldrun, who saw the advantages to having a dragon around to make irritated lords think twice about rebelling against his king. For the many weeks Talon was kept busy visiting and cajoling kings and Barons to consider the advantages of similar unions. With assurances that the dragons would not be used as tools of intimidation, Talon was able to match up ten dragons with reputable castles. Barkin and Fernley jumped at the chance to employ dragons in their respective hobbies. Talon knew the opinions of the other wizards, and didn't bother with offers of dragon cooperation. Talon was pleased with what he had accomplished in so short a time.

Most of the population of the Crinnelian Mountain grudgingly accepted the changes the Krrig Daa was making. But there was a sizable group that felt it was degrading for dragons to be used by humans. A dragon's place was at the top of the food chain and humans were a pleasantly furless appetizer. Talon knew he would never change *their* minds, but hoped that with time his views would be the norm rather than the exception.

## Chapter 12

Life took an alarming turn in early autumn. Graldiss had not yet arrived for morning tea and Talon had just sat down to read Fernley's newest collections of dragon lore and hunting songs when the mountain shook and cave walls screamed. Talon was thrown from his chair, pots and kettles were tossed from their shelves, glass jars and orbs shattered. The air was filled with the sound of released magic.

Talon's mind reached out for answers and was caught in a backlash of pure anger. The random thoughts of fear and panic were overwhelming. Someone, a human, had been in the mountain and taken something. Talon ran into the tunnel and went in search of information. The tunnels were clogged with dragons. He saw no sign of Graldiss and was glad to find Silgaa.

"She's gone!" Silgaa screamed. "They've taken her!"

Talon was confused. "*What's* happened? *Who's* gone?"

"She's gone!" another dragon shouted above the noise. "Someone stole the Queen!"

Panic filled Talon. "The Queen? When?" But when he didn't get any answers. Talon pushed and shoved his way to the hatching cave.

Outside the cave four dragons stood guard. They glared hatefully at him, barring his way. Talon caught a glimpse of the chaos inside. Fifty to sixty dragons flew just above the heads of shouting elders; they were looking intently at the cooling sands, trying to find...something. The cave echoed with the ever rising voices of distressed dragons. Vicious-looking guards stood around the Queen's nest. He was troubled by the overwhelming hatred coming from the cave, hatred aimed at *him*. He returned quickly to the safety of his own cave.

Talon felt helpless. He searched for something he could do, but he didn't even know what had really happened. He called out to Graldiss. There was no immediate answer and he paced around his cave.

When Graldiss came in search of Talon. He was wild with hysteria, shouting and raving in Dragonese. He whipped around the cavern, this tail knocking off anything that hadn't already fallen from the shelves.

Talon caught something about a man sneaking into the mountain, a villainous kidnapping, and

Manett finding the Queen's nest empty. Talon could find nothing to say to his friend. He tried to think rationally. "They wouldn't let me near the hatching cavern. Do they suspect *me*?"

Graldiss nodded. "It was a man, we know that much. The smell was still in the air, and the footprints are clear. A human!" he started to become hysterical again. "After all we've tried to do for your kind! After what we've endured!"

"Do you blame *me*?" Talon stared unbelievingly.

Graldiss opened his mouth, on the verge of another tirade. He closed it tightly and looked helplessly at Talon. "I'm sorry, but I'm upset."

Talon put his hand on his friend's leg. "I am too. If yelling would help, I'd be screaming at the top of my lungs. If turning this mountain inside out would help I'd be the first one with a shovel." Talon paced around the dragon. "What's being done? Have they begun searching at all? Someone must have seen *something*. What can I do?"

Graldiss turned savagely, "*Do*?! You're a *man*! This is *our* business, stay out of it." The speed of the dragon's exit was amazing.

Talon's heart burst into a million pieces. He felt the loss of the Queen and the agony of her subjects. He felt the hatred from all around, even from his best friend. He felt helpless, angry, afraid. He sat down next to the fire pit and wept.

They came for him within the hour. Talon knew two of the four dragons, they were Manett's lackeys. He suspected that the two he didn't know were not fond of him either. None of them looked him in the face. They said nothing, but escorted Talon to the central cavern. Talon hoped to see Graldiss, and was hurt by his absence. Talon was once again brought to the raised dais, but Tollina did not invite him to step up beside her. When Tollina raised her wings the gathered crowd did not completely quiet down. Talon did not like the look of the dragons that sat high on the ledge. Was he going to be the scapegoat? How could they possibly believe that *he* had anything to do with the abduction?

Manett came forward. The assembled dragons fell silent. "As hatchlings we were told stories of the beginning of days, when Dragonkind ruled the world with a firm, but kind claw. We flourished and grew in numbers. Then the vermin that is man crept into our garden." The crowd hissed and jeered. Manett paused and waited until they quieted down. "Mankind was taken under the wings of our innocent ancestors, brought out of the mud and taught the ways of magic. And how were we repaid by those ungrateful creatures?" Again Manett paused and allowed the mob their shouts of anger. "Our naivety brought us misery and death." From all over the cavern names of murdered family members were shouted out. "Once again we have brought a human into our midst." Boo's and hisses made clear their emotions. Manett did not wait for the commotion to die down, but raised her voice louder with each point of her argument. "We have welcomed this human as if he were one of us. In her innocence, our greatest Matriarch has given him her power. And how are we repaid? The vermin has crept amongst us and stolen our most precious Queen. Will we sit idly by and allow this to go unpunished?" The roars of outrage were deafening.

The crowd pressed in. The only thing standing between Talon and the razor sharp claws were his four guards. Talon could have translocated himself away from the fate Manett clearly had in store for him, but that would only reinforce the accusations. Better to stay and die than justify Manett's accusations.

Tollina tried to quiet the hysterical mob and even took steps to protect Talon. "Surely the Krrig Daa deserves the right to plead his innocence."

Manett raised her wing and the cave fell deathly silent. "Innocence? Can any human be innocent?!" Fire and smoke filled the air.

"This one is." From high above the cavern a stream of dragons flew through the ceiling hole, Graldiss in the lead. The dragons hovered over the dais, Graldiss landed firmly next to Talon, pushing Manett out of the way. "Rushing things a bit, aren't you councilor? I thought that you would be the first dragon out looking for our Queen." Graldiss' voice was loud enough for the whole cavern to hear. "If you had been, you would have discovered what we have." The angry mob fell silent, listening. "It was indeed a human who came into the hatching cave and stole away our Queen. But he had black hair." All eyes turned to Talon's white hair. "And he had no power over magic. The villain walked heavily, at least 20-stone heavier than the Krrig Daa."

Murmurs began to rise throughout the crowd. Manett saw her power over them slipping. "I don't know where you got your information, but do you have proof that *this* human did not take part in the abduction? We all know the history between the two of you, don't you think that you may be biased."

Silgaa swooped low. "Because we know the path that was taken down the mountain, and we have details from the grass and the rocks." The crowd began to step back from Talon, looking confused. "And it was revealed that a dragon took part in the theft." A cry of outrage filled the air.

Manett stood her ground. "All the more reason to suspect the Chosen One. He has great influence over the weak-minded. He is a cunning wizard." Heads nodded acknowledging the point. Manett stressed his point, "Remember, he is a *human!*"

"No, he became one of us when Magrid gave him the power of a dragon." Graldiss spoke quietly, but was heard throughout the cavern.

Graldiss looked to Tollina for the voice of reason. Tollina raised her wings and called for silence. "With the evidence revealed to us, and the unflinching behavior of the man standing here accused, I call for an end to this rebellious mob. Let us turn our energies to the real task before us." Tollina looked down at Talon with a smile of relief. "Please forgive our rash behavior."

Talon returned the smile but said nothing. He walked slowly out of the cavern. Dragons moved aside to make way for him. Graldiss did not immediately follow, but remained behind to help organize search parties. When Graldiss arrived at Talon's cave he found the wizard slumped in his chair by the fire. "I am sorry," Graldiss said softly.

Talon turned to look at his friend. "Sorry? You saved my neck, why should you apologize?"

"This morning I might have joined that pack of jackals. I wasn't thinking clearly."

Talon nodded. "I wouldn't have blamed you. I'm just glad that you were able to find some evidence to help me out." He motioned for his friend to join him by the fire pit. "Was there anything else you could get from the grass? They usually like to give every detail if given the chance."

"They claim that the dragon who led the thief out of the mountain was an elder, whose legs were orange." Graldiss gladly accepted a round of cheese. "I have my suspicions, but with my intimate relationship to you, I think it would be best to step back and let others look into conspiracies."

Talon had to agree. He would have to be very careful about any accusations he made. "Will they allow me to help search for Ittra? I feel so helpless just sitting here."

"I think Tollina shamed them into accepting any help you can offer. She has asked that you not consult any of the other wizards, though."

"No, you wouldn't want it known that someone can just walk in and take the Queen egg out from under our noses." Talon stared into the flames. He freed his mind and let it roam through the tunnels. A gentle hum from the walls followed along. Talon kept his thoughts away from individual caves, drifting through the public caverns and into the hatching cave. In the large open cave Talon let his mind float high above the sands, not focusing on any one thing. He reached for the power Magrid had given him and replayed the events of that morning.

At sunrise the clutches of eggs were shifted and the sands groomed by an elderly red dragon. Tollina came in a short while later and polished Ittra's egg. They chatted for a few minutes then Tollina left. From a seldom used side tunnel, two dark shapes came into view. They stayed in the tunnel for some time talking. Talon focused his attention there; he slid time back again and listened to their conversation.

"He will be gone soon, be patient."

"How many more of you will come and go before we can do what we came for?"

Talon had no trouble recognizing the voices; he had a harder time believing that a dragon who so hated humans would conspire with a human that hated dragons even more.

"He will be the last," the dragon said.

"Good. I don't want to be here any longer than I have to," the man's voice was full of venom.

"It is heavier than you might think," the dragon informed the thief.

"I can handle it. You just make sure I have a head start before that freak comes after me."

"I can handle him."

Talon withdrew his mind from the cave. He didn't need to see any more. It didn't matter how Keldric carried Ittra out or which exit from the mountain he took. What mattered was getting her back.

Graldiss looked intently at Talon. He knew the boy had sent his mind out wandering, and was anxious to hear what he discovered. He had his own ideas about the human involved, but he didn't want to even consider which dragon assisted in the plot.

Talon opened his eyes and took a couple of deep breaths. He was exhausted. Graldiss brought Talon a cup of hot cider. Talon took the cup gratefully, his hands shook. After a few minutes he felt strong enough to stand. "Can you take me to that path outside the mountain? I can't hear the Queen from in here."

Graldiss transported them both to the path outside a well-hidden opening in the mountainside. "We think they came in this way." Any traces of footprints were destroyed by the zealous searchers.

Talon nodded, "Yes. The dragon waited for Keldric and led him inside." He looked down the rough path and held out his hands. He didn't normally feel it necessary to use gestures when using magic, but he felt he could use all the extra help he could get. Talon's mind called out to any animals that might have seen anything. He was jolted by the number of answering thoughts that streamed into him. "One at a time, please."

After a moment's pause an eagle spoke, "It is a fine morning; the air is warm and the fish slow. You are anxious."

"Thank you for your concern. I am looking for a man who traveled down from the mountain since sunrise."

"The air is cool above the mountain and the rabbits are fast. I saw a man, but he smelled of dragon, confusing. He went into the trees, I saw him no more."

"Thank you. Fly high, hunt well." Talon felt lucky that the eagle wanted to discuss something other than the day's hunting. Other thoughts took their turn. Talon convinced the grass to give him a condensed version of the grand story of a man who climbed the dragon-mountain by foot, entered the secret passage and came out with a rare package. Various animals chatted about their nests, the best trees for nuts, the cleverness of escaping an owl, and cautioned Talon not to trust a patch of hungry sand by the fallen pine. But none of the creatures strayed near the mountain path or saw a man descending the mountain. Though there was a lot of talk about the morning's abundance of dragons making noise. One brave mouse suggested Talon return in the evening and speak to a brown owl that had been hunting in the area early in the morning.

Talon started down the path. He didn't get far before he realized there was nothing more he would learn from the rocks and bushes. He knew Keldric had come up the mountain before sunrise, and came back down with the egg before the morning dew had left the leaves. "Graldiss, do you know where this path comes out below?"

The dragon bent low and extended his leg. "Climb up, I'll take you."

Talon accepted the offer. He didn't really like flying on dragons; there was very little to hold on to that wouldn't slice his hands and his legs would never be long enough to wrap totally around the neck. Talon doubted Graldiss would allow him to fashion a saddle for such trips. It *was* the quickest way to get anywhere, it just didn't seem natural. As a soldier, Talon had learned how to read the traffic that had passed along a road the previous day. From the sky Talon could read nothing.

Graldiss set Talon down in front of a thick forest. This was as far as the search parties had gone. Talon looked around; there were visible signs that someone entered the forest recently. He spoke to a bramble bush near the path and learned that a man had passed by earlier in the morning. It was a sure bet that it was Keldric. But what was not a sure bet was whether Keldric traveled straight through the forest or had taken a different path out. "Graldiss, fly to the other side of this forest and see if you can find where Keldric came out." The dragon nodded and flew off.

Talon sat down on the path and cleared his thoughts. He softly called out to the Queen, no sense alerting the whole world that she was missing. He listened carefully. The answer came instantly.

"Good morning, Talon. Where am I?"

Relief filled the young wizard. "I don't know. I'm trying to find you."

"I'm hot. I was cold when I woke, and now I'm so hot. What has happened?" The Queen sounded confused, but not afraid.

"You were taken from the hatching cave. We are all looking for you."

"Taken?" There was a pause before she asked, "Who is this dark man?"

"Dark? His skin is dark?"

"No, silly. I can't see what he looks like. His mind is dark, closed off to me. He is filled with anger."

Talon smiled, that about summed up Keldric. "He is an old foe of mine." Talon sent Ittra images of his history with the once wizard. "I'm not sure what his motives for taking you are, yet."

"Well I don't like him. Come and get me." The Queen was beginning to sound like a little child who wanted to stop playing a game.

"Can you tell me where you are?"

After another pause Ittra answered. "I'm in a large box near flames. The trees are damaged and don't like to talk."

Talon puzzled at her description. They had not seen a fire from the sky. "Can you transport back to the cave?"

"No, something here is keeping me locked here." The Queen paused. "A mouse tells me that the man has a big shiny stick, a sword, and he's making it sharp."

"I think he's going to try to crack your egg." Talon warned.

Ittra's laugh was a ray of hope. "That's silly; my egg is too hard for a human to break."

"Keldric must have put you near a fire."

"Keldric, is that the dark man's name? I don't like it. How did he take me from the mountain?"

"He snuck in through a hidden tunnel and stole you away." Talon didn't want to mention the help Keldric had gotten.

Graldiss landed near Talon. "There is no sign of Keldric's exit. He must still be in the forest, or has taken another path." The dragon's expression was a mix of fear and hatred. "It could take days to find him."

"The Queen is safe for now. I have been able to talk with her. I think Keldric will try to break her out of her shell." Talon stood and dusted the leaves from his legs. "The trees are too close to allow dragons to enter, and he may think that I'm no longer a threat. So he won't be looking for me."

Graldiss was frustrated that he couldn't do anything to help his Queen. "What should I tell the others?"

"Tell them I've gone to rescue our Queen. I will not come back without her." Talon entered the forest.

Talon found it easy to track Keldric through the trees. The extra weight of the dragon egg made his footprints very clear. Talon spoke with the Queen often as he followed a side path and crossed a creek.

"I'm not so hot, now. He must have taken me away from the fire."

Talon decided that Keldric must be in a building of some kind. Ittra didn't mention speaking to any birds or rocks.

"He's banging something on my shell. Why is he trying to hatch me?"

Talon didn't answer right away. "My guess is that he wants your power. Keldric saw how strong I became after receiving Magrid's power. I'm sure he was almost insane after I removed his own power, he'd do anything to get it back, and to get back at me."

"Get back at you?"

"What better way to discredit me with dragons? Many already think I had something to do with the theft." Another side path and a fallen tree, Talon knew by the clarity of Ittra's thoughts that he was getting nearer.

"Now he's trying to cut. This man's not too bright. I don't think he could have planned to steal me without help. Who was it?"

"We don't know for certain," Talon lied.

Ittra knew this was not true, but did not pursue the matter. "What would their reason be? Who wants to take my place? Who do I threaten? Why did they accuse you?"

"A human stole you, and I'm a human. Hate one and it's easier to hate them all." Talon knew the young Queen would soon decide who had the most to gain from her disappearance and his removal. He added another angle. "If anything should happen to you, there would be another war between dragons and humans. If I'm out of the way that's one less wizard to deal with."

Ittra agreed. "Then you'd better get me back. Wait, there's a dragon here now." A sense of relief filled her thoughts. "Wait, she's guarding her mind, I can't see who it is."

The Queen's uncertainty worried Talon and he began to run. He ordered the trees to move their branches aside and relocated rocks out of his way.

"The dragon is trying to use magic to weaken my shell."

Talon no longer needed to check for tracks, Ittra's mind was a beacon for him, and he knew he couldn't be far off now.

"Please hurry, this dragon is very smart."

Talon ran faster, he no longer felt the whipping and scratching of branches. A rough trapping cabin came into view. Talon pulled in energy from everything around him. "Hold on!" Talon released the power in one large burst. The walls of the cabin blew apart.

In the dust and debris, Talon saw a silhouette of a dragon as it grabbed Keldric and transported away. He heard Keldric's shout of frustration before they disappeared.

Talon rushed to Ittra's side. "Are you alright?" He stroked the undamaged shell.

"You were a bit extreme."

Talon laughed with relief. He looked around, hoping that he was mistaken and Keldric's body was buried under the rubble. All he found was the ashes of a dead fire and an assortment of weapons and tools Keldric was using to try to break the Queen's egg. Talon calmed his rage. "They're gone."

"I'm surprised they weren't blown to bits. You were awfully rough."

"I didn't think it was a time for subtly."

"But you gave them the chance to escape without seeing who the dragon was."

Talon was hurt by the Queen's scolding. "Forgive me, I was on the edge."

Ittra giggled and Talon felt forgiven. "I'm getting cold. Can we go home now?"

Talon called out for Graldiss. He told his friend he had the Queen safe and would return them both to his cave. He put his arms around the egg and pictured a spot near the foot of his bed. In an instant he was able to lay the egg on the soft mattress.

Graldiss arrived only moments after Talon. He went to the bed and checked the egg. "I'm fine, Small One. But your friend might need some looking after."

Graldiss carried the exhausted Talon to his chair. "Thank you."

"They'll come soon." Talon tried to stand back up. "She needs to go back to the hatching cave. If they find her here they will think—"

"They will think what I *tell* them to think. After today I don't feel safe in the hatching cave. I feel safe here."

Tollina was the first to arrive. She rushed to the egg and brushed the dirt away. Manett came soon after, pushing through the crowd that filled the tunnel. Graldiss moved protectively in front of Ittra.

"This is no proper place for our Queen," Manett said, and with a wave of her claw the egg disappeared.

Talon jumped from his chair and would have thrown himself at Manett if Silgaa had not caught him in mid-leap. "Where is she?" Talon hissed.

"Our Queen will rest peacefully on her nest in the hatching grounds." Manett turned to leave, but the reappearance of Ittra's egg on the bed stopped her in mid-stride. She turned and glared at Talon. "How *dare* you."

"Watch your tone, Manett; you are speaking to the Krrig Daa." Ittra's voice was cold.

Manett was silent. By the look on the other dragons' faces, Talon realized that everyone had heard the Queen's voice. It was very evident this was the first time the Queen had spoken to the whole population. Talon stood tall.

"This human rescued me when no dragon could. My thanks are unbounded. Just because of the evil deeds of one human, we will not condemn them all. Do not let this incident turn us from the work the

Krrig Daa has set before us. For now I will remain here until safer quarters can be arranged." Her words were the final say in the matter. Manett transported out of Talon's cave without another word.

"She has to go." Talon paced around the cave, trying to formulate a plan.

Ittra knew the meaning behind Talon's words. "No," she said calmly.

Talon pulled a chair next to the bed and sat down. "She can't be trusted. You *know* she arranged to have you kidnapped. What's to say she won't try something like that again?"

"I will handle it."

The softness in the Queen's voice confused Talon. He had seen great power within her mind, but she was still just a baby. It was possible that she didn't understand the seriousness of the situation. "As a soldier I learned never to leave an enemy behind, especially one as powerful as Manett. I will have to kill her."

"No, you can't."

"She will fight us at every turn," Talon explained. "Her hatred for me is all consuming, and she has no love for you, either. She'll be trouble."

"And do you think she's the only one that hates? If you rid yourself of one enemy, another will rise up to take their place. I thought you have also learned *that* as a soldier."

Talon felt the sting of Ittra's reprimand, but he had to admit the truth of her words.

"I understand your feelings of distrust toward Manett," Ittra continued, "and admit that I share some of those feelings. But even if she were the only one to object to your presence I would still not allow you to kill her."

"Why not?"

Ittra words were almost too quiet to hear: "Because you are a human. No matter how noble your reasoning, no matter how much dragon power you carry in your mind; you will be a human killing a dragon, and that's all that will be remembered."

Talon didn't want to admit defeat. "Then let a dragon do the deed. Graldiss suspects Manett's role in your kidnapping. If I explain it to him, I'm sure—"

"Don't you dare ask that sweet beast to do such a thing."

The Queen's harsh words made Talon feel guilty. "I'm sorry. You're right, of course." Talon was disappointed that he would not have his revenge. He wanted to kick something.

Ittra laughed. "You are such a child. I may still be in my egg, but I have *some* authority. I will arrange everything." She giggled. "I think I will arrange something for you as well."

Talon didn't trust the Queen's tone.

Within a week the Queen held council in the hatching cave. Graldiss was stunned to be included. For the first time Tollina didn't take center stage, but stood next to Ittra's egg. The confused council members were surprised when Ittra spoke to them.

"The time has come for me to take a more active role in matters of my colony."

Annol, one of Manett's supporters, stepped forward. "I beg your pardon, but how can you rule while unhatched?"

"It is true that I am choosing to stay within-egg, I do not feel physically prepared to hatch. There is the precedence of Queen Niann, who stayed within-egg for fifty years, and ruled during forty of them. I will hatch when I feel ready. Until then I will hold council here."

No one was brave enough to openly oppose the Queen. They did, however, object to the inclusion of Graldiss. "It cannot be denied that this fine young dragon played a key role in the prophecy of the Krrig Daa. But he is not an elder nor has he demonstrated the leadership skills required by this position."

"Thank you, Manett. I am well aware of Graldiss' qualifications and which ones he lacks. But during the recent crisis, this dragon kept a cool head on his neck and kept a bad situation from becoming a catastrophe. I have spoken to him at length, and feel he would be a valuable addition to the council. If you feel that he needs some training, Manett, why don't you take him under your wing and see to it that he knows everything he needs to know."

With that handled, Ittra spoke to the rest of the members of the council. "I will be choosing my own guards in the next few days. Please send me your best young dragons for my consideration."

Later that evening, when Ittra told Talon of the meeting he realized the Queen had more grit than he gave her credit for. He was going to have to reevaluate his opinion of this young Queen.

# Chapter 13

“Talon! Come quick!”

Talon rolled over and pulled the covers over his head. “It’s too early to feed the goats,” he mumbled. A stab of pain brought him fully awake and he opened his eyes. A quick check of his limbs assured him that it was not his own pain he felt.

“You must hurry!” Ittra’s voice was near panic. “Don’t use magic, run!”

Talon didn’t ask any questions, but took off at a dead run. He cursed softly when he stubbed his toe and again when he forgot a turn in the tunnel and slammed into the hard stone. He was out of breath and bleeding when he entered the softly lit hatching cave. As he stood, catching his breath, Talon was hit with a wave of fear and panic. “Ittra?! What’s wrong? Are you hurt?”

“Not me,” she said softly. The magic release of her thoughts gently blended with the background magic of a mountain full of dragons. "One of the clutches is dying."

Talon felt the wave of panic again and he moved toward the many clusters of eggs. "Which one?"

"I can't tell. Near a tunnel, I think, there's a breeze."

Four tunnels opened into the hatching cave. Talon peered through the dim light, looking for a cluster nearest to one of them. After a moment he found what he was looking for and ran to the far side of the cavern. His heart sank when he saw one of the eggs had fallen over and broken open. The infant dragon had smothered in the sand.

Ittra saw the horror through Talon's eyes. "Poor thing. But she is not the only one. When one clutchmate dies, the others follow, from fear or shock. There is only one left. You need to keep him alive."

Unsure of what he should do, Talon put his hand on each egg, feeling for some sign that the infant dragon was alive. The first one he touched was cold and silent. The second was cold, but there was a sobbing inside. Talon flung his arms around the egg. "I'm here," was all he could think of saying.

"They're gone!" The small mind inside wailed. "It's so quiet."

"Stay with me. Don't give in to the fear." Sympathetic tears rolled down Talon's face. The darkness coming from the egg was awful. "What do I do?" he asked Ittra.

"First you've got to get it out of here. They'll come soon, and kill him."

Talon was too worried to question the Queen. He wrapped his arms around the egg and pulled it from the sand. Carrying it in his arms would be too awkward. He took off his shirt, wrapped the egg inside and swung it over his shoulder. As quickly as he could, Talon returned to his cave reassuring the infant dragon along the way.

Once in his own cave, Talon lit the fire and placed the egg far from the flames. "You'll be safe here."

"It's so quiet. They're gone." The voice was fading.

Talon risked the noise of the magic and sent his mind into the egg. He'd never been in a mind so young, or so close to death. Fear, confusion and loneliness overwhelmed him. "I'm here, and I won't leave. I know your clutchmates are gone, you don't need to go with them."

"Emik was just trying to wiggle his tail." The panic Talon felt earlier was beginning to subside. "He couldn't breathe." Talon saw a vision of a baby dragon, still wet, struggling weakly to right himself. "Janaa was so upset and she went away right after Emik." Talon saw that Janaa's essence faded so quickly it couldn't be stopped. "Geddig was quiet. He said we couldn't make it without Emik and Janaa.

She said we should both go, before anyone could worry about us. Geddig was always saying things like that. She knew the *dragon-way*. She thought I would follow after her. But it was so dark, and cold. I was afraid."

"It was very brave to hang on when your friends had gone. And now you are no longer alone."

The baby dragon seemed to accept Talon's reassurances. He was tired. "Will it be alright if I sleep?"

Talon withdrew from the small mind. "Sleep. I'll watch over you." He was relieved that he no longer felt thoughts of dying. He pushed dirt up around the base of the egg. Talon reached out for Ittra. She didn't speak directly to him, but allowed him to hear what she was saying to someone else.

"It couldn't have been helped. The egg toppled over and the poor thing was dead before I could call out for anyone." Talon did not hear the dragon's response. "Agnar is safe. I would not have him give up his life." Ittra became angry with something the other had said. "Are you lecturing me on dragon law? It was *my* choice," she said with finality. "Care for the others and return tomorrow." She put an end to the conversation and waited until the other left before speaking to Talon. "How is he?"

"Sad, and a bit guilty for not dying." Talon pushed his comfortable chair next to the egg.

He had dug into the memories that Magrid had given him to try and understand what had happened. He saw that the clutch was all important. The clutch-bonds remained throughout the life of a dragon. Centuries ago a female dragon would lay a single egg and sit with it until the hatching, and then care for the baby until it was able to hunt on its own. But with the horror of the war with the humans things changed. More eggs had to be laid to ensure the survival of the species, and the mothers could not remain with their eggs. Instead, the elder dragons would cluster the eggs together in groups of four. The baby dragons would keep each other company, freeing up the adults to fight for their survival. The bonding within a clutch was so strong that many clutchmates stayed together in adulthood. If anything should happen to cause one of the clutchmates to die while still within the egg the shock and loss always seemed to lead to the deaths of the rest of the clutch.

Over a hundred years ago a baby dragon was orphaned after a minor cave-in took the lives of several clutches. Attempts were made to include the lone egg with other clutches, but their bonds were already firm, and the fifth was rejected time and again. In the end the single egg was left on its own until hatching. After hatching the orphaned youngling fared no better. The other younglings did not always mean to neglect Vettrik. They just didn't always remember to include him in their games. With time the youngling stopped trying to fit in and isolated himself. As Vettrik grew he began to behave irrationally, lashing out for no apparent reason. In the end, the elders judged Vettrik to be mentally unstable, and the young dragon had to be killed. The lack of the close-knit unit was blamed for the deviance. A second incident involving an orphaned dragon confirmed the judgment. It became generally accepted that it would be more merciful to take the life of any survivor of a failed clutch.

"Then why save this one?" Talon asked Ittra.

"Because I think they were wrong. I didn't see anything in Agnar that would indicate he would become mentally unstable, in fact, quite the opposite."

Talon laid his hand on the warming egg. He knew what the Queen wanted him to do, but he wanted to hear it from her. "And where do I fit into this?"

"Why, as savior, of course. That's your job title, isn't it? I will handle the brunt of the objections, but you may have to make some changes in your life."

Talon laughed, it seemed making adjustments was all he did since he met Olwin. He considered the situation. There didn't seem to be any likelihood that the dragons would accept this Agnar, and they weren't going to appreciate his involvement in the matter. He was pretty sure he was going to make even more enemies than he already had. Well who said life with dragons was going to be easy? "What ever you say." After a while Talon dozed lightly.

"What is *that* doing here?!"

Talon jerked himself awake and glared at Graldiss. "Be quiet, will you. Agnar needs to sleep."

Graldiss opened his mouth but could think of nothing to say and closed it again. Of course he had heard about the poor dragonet that died and his clutch that followed him. But he had not heard about *this.* He quickly ran through all the imaginable possibilities as to why Talon was sitting next to one of the eggs. "This isn't right," was all he could think to say.

"It wasn't my idea. But I think I have to agree with the Queen. One demented dragon is no basis to kill an innocent baby. If he's not treated like an outsider the little beast should be fine. Why can't he be added to another clutch, or cared for by a nice set of parental-type dragons?"

"Because it just isn't *done.*" Graldiss knew how weak this sounded, but how else could he explain it to a human. "You must accept it."

"Well Ittra isn't going to accept it, and I don't think I can either." Talon put some wood on the fire. "Are you going to tell me you can't accept that a small dragon would choose life over death? Is that so unnatural?"

"That's the way it's been. Some things must be accepted without question."

Talon turned his frustration directly at his friend. "Do you know how stupid that sounds? You would kill a helpless baby because of what happened a hundred years ago?! Without any evidence that he is anything but a normal dragon who doesn't want to sacrifice himself just because his clutchmates have died."

"I'm sorry, but that's the way it is."

The dragon's calm acceptance was too much to take. Talon stamped his foot. "Then I'm surprised I'm here to have this silly conversation with you." Graldiss looked confused. "If you're going to stand there and tell me some things need to be accepted without question then I wonder why you didn't make a meal of me the first time we met. Surely you can't tell me it's natural to become friends with a *human*?" Graldiss looked away. "And after a century of war between humans and dragons here, I stand in the midst of a bloody horde of you. There are thirty dragons are out there living with humans." Talon moved right up to the large dragon's face and poked the scaly chest. "You can't have it both ways, either live in the past or help create the future. Either way, I'm not letting anyone get near this egg." Talon stood back and held out his hand threateningly. "Interfere with me and I'll shrink you back down to the size of a cat." He smiled mischievously. "You *know* I can do it, I'm the most powerful wizard alive."

Graldiss was relieved at the break in tension. "I might get a terrible case of indigestion, but I could eat you in one bite." The dragon plopped down next to the egg. "You're not going to get off lightly for this." He tapped the egg with a claw. "You awake in there?"

"Yes," Agnar said meekly. "Are you going to kill me now?"

Talon wanted to hear the answer too.

"Well, not right now." Graldiss sat down. "What happened last night?"

Agnar told Graldiss about Emik. "I felt awful. Janaa couldn't take it. It was worse to feel her die than Emik. I think I would have died for her, but it was Geddig that changed my mind. All his talk about duty and necessity made me mad. He didn't *care* about Emik's or Janaa's death, only that we follow the *tradition* and die with them."

Graldiss had to admit this little unhatched dragon had guts. "But now you're alone."

"The other one said I wouldn't be alone," Agnar said defiantly.

Talon put his hand on the egg. "And you won't be. My name's Talon, you can stay with me."

"Are you really a *wizard*? Wizards are supposed to be evil. Why are you living with us?"

"That's a long story. I'll tell you some day. But for now I think you should sleep, and I will consider what to do next."

"You won't let him kill me, will you?"

Graldiss looked sheepishly at Talon. "You are safe, little one," he said. "You have nothing to fear from me." Agnar seemed satisfied with this answer and slept. "And I guess I won't *eat* you today either." He sighed heavily. "How is it you always seem to get your way?"

Talon leaned against his friend. "I'm the Chosen One," he said dramatically. "What do I do now?"

The dragon had to laugh. "*I'm* supposed to get you out of this mess? Why not ask the Queen, she's the one who got you into it."

Ittra did what she could to calm the angry elders. Most of the younger dragons, like Graldiss, grudgingly accepted her decision on the lone clutchling. But there was a large faction that refused to have their laws circumvented with no discussion. It didn't help that Talon had been involved. Manett was quick to imply that the human had something to do with their Queen's decision.

Talon did not like the atmosphere of resentment that was beginning to invade the mountain. A week after he had brought the egg into his life, Talon made the decision to move out of the mountain.

"My presence is doing neither of us any good," he told the Queen. "I've gain a lot of ground toward better human/dragon relations with the younger dragons. My leaving won't change that. But I'm a constant reminder to the elder dragons that things aren't as they were and I'm hoping my leaving will help ease the tension."

Ittra had her own reasons for agreeing with Talon's decision. "I'm afraid of what prejudices the youngling will face if he stays here. He's lost so much already, he shouldn't have to be reminded of it everyday."

Talon made arrangements for a cottage to be built in a meadow below the mountain. He was saddened that Graldiss wasn't leaving with him. Talon understood his friend had more responsibility as a member of the council, but he would miss their late night singing and friendly fights. Talon felt like he was leaving a brother.

Graldiss couldn't see what all the fuss was about. "You're not moving to a desert island, though there are dragons who would like that. Will it make you feel better if I promise to come and visit every night and sing you to sleep?"

"Oh would you?" Graldiss threw a book at Talon's grinning face. Talon easily diverted it to a packing crate. "I will be depending on you to help me with Agnar. I might have the memories of a dragon, but I don't know the first thing about the mechanics of flight, or the intricacies of hunting."

"You want me to be his big brother, is that it?"

"Yes, I suppose I do. You don't mind, do you?"

Graldiss heaved a dramatic sigh. "I guess not, but I refuse to be the one that has to tell him the facts of life."

"I'll get Kaalla to do that." Talon finished packing his things. "I'll miss this place. The hum of the walls was very soothing."

"You won't stay away forever." Graldiss helped Talon carry the last of his belongings. Talon transported himself and Graldiss next to his cottage.

Talon found Agnar's egg being cuddled by Kaalla. "What a sweet little thing, and so brave."

"He's got hard times ahead," Graldiss said, scratching the drowsy egg. "He'll need that bravery." The dragon turned to Talon. "I'll come tomorrow, if you wish."

"You know you're welcome anytime, old friend." Talon held back his tears. "I expect you to keep me up on all the news from the mountain." He watched in silence as Graldiss rose into the sky and disappeared.

Kaalla handed Agnar's egg to Talon. "I think that young dragon might be a bit jealous of your new charge."

This was something Talon hadn't thought of. "You may be right. Do you have any advice?"

The elderly dragon patted Talon on the cheek. "This baby will need a lot of attention, but don't neglect your friends and take time for yourself." She blinked out of sight.

Talon had hoped for something more substantial. He carried Agnar inside and placed the egg on a mound of cool sand. He looked around, and with a sigh, began to unpack. As he moved around the cottage, Talon realized this was the first time he had been on his own in many years. It felt odd.

"You aren't alone," a tiny voice said from inside Talon's head.

Talon went to the egg and rubbed it. "You are so right. We will keep each other company." He put a pot of cider on the hearth.

Talon stood in the cold autumn air watching four dragons fly away. They had come to report on their progress with a farming community north of Needam.

"It seems the advantage of dragon-fire has not gone unnoticed," Talon told the egg as he prepared supper. "Controlled burning of wheat fields was a good idea. Soon every farming community will want a dragon. And the nobles have benefited by their flying messengers."

"How soon will you be able to teach *me* to fly, Talon?"

"I can't fly, remember. Graldiss will teach you. I'm told if you dry your wings by the fire after you hatch you should be strong enough within a day to make short flights."

"I could be flying *tomorrow*?!" The egg wobbled with excitement.

"Calm down! You'll fall over and be no better off than Emik. You have to hatch before you can fly, silly."

"OK."

Talon jumped at the first crack. "I didn't mean *now*!" Talon panicked as four more cracks appeared on the surface of the shaking egg.

"This is harder than I thought it would be." With a grunt Agnar stuck his foot through the egg. The tiny, clawed toes wiggled and stretched. It didn't take long before the baby dragon lay among the shards of shell. Big green eyes squinted in the fire light. The near transparent blue wings hung damply on the glistening ridges that would become spines.

Talon laughed as the brown baby dragon the size of a full-grown spaniel stretched and twisted in front of the fire. He picked up the bits of shell before Agnar ground them into the rug.

Agnar stood shakily on his legs, fell over twice, then tottered across to Talon. "I'm hungry!" the tiny voice squeaked.

A small piece of ham appeared in Talon's hand. He held a chunk out. Small razor sharp teeth carefully took the meat from Talon's hand.

"Ick!" The half-chewed chunk was spit out onto the floor. "What *was* that?"

"Sorry, I don't have anything raw. Can you make do with an apple until morning?"

"What's an apple?" Talon held out his hand and a red apple replaced the offensive ham. After a hesitant nibble the little dragon finished off the apple in two bites. As he licked his lips Agnar studied Talon. "You don't look like I thought you would. Taller, and skinnier. Are you sure you're only supposed to have two legs?"

Talon ignored the question. "You're a bit bigger than I expected." Talon sat on the floor. "It must have been a tight fit in that egg."

"Very." Agnar unfolded his wings and stretched them out to the warm flames. "It feels so good to stretch out." The baby dragon extended his neck and spread his toes, the skinny tail whipped around and thumped on the floor. The paper-thin wings slowly stretched open to their fullest. A bit of pink tongue showed as a few tentative flaps were tried. With a disappointed sigh Agnar folded the useless wings.

"Did you expect to go zooming around the room? I told you it would take a bit of time. Try again in the morning."

Agnar had to be satisfied with a wobbly run around the room, stopping only to spread his wings to dry in the flames for a moment before running off again. When he was exhausted, the baby dragon dropped in a heap by the fire. Within minutes he was snoring happily.

The next morning Graldiss was welcomed warmly by an eager Agnar. "Are you my big brother? Will you take me out flying? I've dried my wings and practiced flapping. Can we go hunting? Talon tried to feed me some awful meat called haamm. Don't you think it's funny the way he walks on two feet? He can't fly, you know."

Graldiss scowled at the energetic young dragon. "Be respectful of your elders, youngling. Talon is a very important human; we do not laugh at his shortcomings." He looked Agnar over. "You are smaller than I thought you would be. Stretch out your wings."

Agnar unfurled his wings flapping them for good measure. His small body lifted off of the ground a few inches. "I'm hungry."

"Of course you are, younglings are always hungry. At your size what do you expect to hunt, mice? I will hunt, you will watch." Graldiss disappeared. Agnar looked around, confused. "Outside, youngling," Graldiss called to the baby dragon's mind.

When Talon returned from his errands he found Agnar asleep in the shade of the apple tree, Graldiss lounging beside him. Talon pulled off an apple and joined them. "How did it go? He seems pretty content."

"I had forgotten how active younglings are. Once I showed him the basics of flight I couldn't get him back on the ground. I'll say this, he'll keep the area clear of rats and mice. Younglings have huge appetites."

Talon looked over at Agnar, who had rolled onto his back with his feet sticking in the air. "How fast will he grow?"

"Hard to tell. Normal younglings reach their full size in three years, but who knows what differences there'll be without a clutch." Graldiss lowered his voice, "He doesn't seem to exhibit any abnormal tendencies...yet."

Talon felt frustrated, if Graldiss had reservations about Agnar, would *any* dragon accept him? He stood and went into the cottage.

Over the next few weeks, before the frost set in, Graldiss came by to instruct the young dragon. Agnar was a quick learner and delighted in swooping around the cabin, stalking and pouncing on Talon's ears and toes. As the nights grew long Talon trained the youngling on the use of magic. Magrid's memories of basic dragon magic came in handy.

Swooping and hunting took turns with translocating cushions and forming glowing balls of light. During the long winter evenings Talon and Agnar played a form of catch; magically throwing a ball, stopping it in mid flight and tossing it back. Agnar's favorite practical joke was to drop a damp towel on Talon after the lights had been extinguished. It soon became a game: Talon would relocate himself and Agnar would track him down and drop the towel on him. Talon didn't mind getting wet a few times if it honed the youngling's abilities.

Before long Agnar's grasp of magic surpassed that of younglings twice his age. And because Agnar spent all of his time around Talon and Graldiss, he seemed more mature.

Graldiss was assigned to look for signs of an unstable mind in the youngling. Manett was sure that the orphaned dragon must have a seed of darkness just waiting to take root and she wanted someone there when the first tendril came to light. Graldiss suspected that Manett, who still resented his inclusion into the council, just wanted him out of the way. Sending him to watch over Agnar was an excuse to get rid of him.

## Chapter 14

As the mid-winter full moon approached Talon began to make preparations for the Hatching Festival. The event had the potential to be very exciting. Thousands of dragons from all over the world gathered at a secret location known only to dragon queens. Once a year the separate queens transported their whole colony to celebrate the birth of every dragon. When he learned of the event from Magrid's memories, Talon thought it rather typical of dragons to celebrate all of their birthdays at one time. But the event wasn't just a birthday party; it was a time to exchange news, meet distant relatives, and to make a full counting of their kind. The task of transporting so many dragons was a trial of a queen's power. Even in-egg queens were judged by how many and how quickly her dragons arrived at the site. This was also a time when dragons showed off their many talents in skills of magic, strength, and speed.

Talon taught Agnar to juggle light balls in mid-air. The bright youngling began to add detail and definition to the shining spheres until he could change their shape and color several times a cycle. Talon perfected his sheep-eye marmalade, and spent weeks baking the large loaves of bread he would need to make toast points.

Ittra had spoken to Talon about their allotted space in the transport schedule. To keep the shock to a minimum, Talon would travel with a contingent of his followers, and Tollina. She had been in contact with the other queens and had informed them of Talon's special connection to dragons. She expected there to be quite a stir over his and Agnar's inclusion, from her own dragons as well as the majority of the other colonies. She asked Talon to prepare Agnar for this.

Agnar was smart enough to understand that he was not accepted by most of the dragons in the mountain that loomed above their home, and he knew why. He had heard the story of Vettrik, the first orphaned clutchling who had been so traumatized by his loneliness that in a jealous rage he killed all of the clutches in the hatching cavern. A second orphaned dragon, a decade later, had turned traitor during the human/dragon war and helped a vicious knight gain entrance to the colony where he slaughtered 30 dragons before both of them were killed. Talon had explained the psychological damage the orphaned dragons had experienced from not belonging to a clutch, the lack of bonding and clutch-friendships that an orphan is deprived of. But Agnar did not feel such a deprivation. It was true that he missed his clutchmates terribly, and some nights cried himself to sleep, but since he had not mixed with other dragons his age, Agnar had not grown jealous of their closeness. In fact, Agnar felt lucky to have the sole attention of an adult dragon. Yes, he knew Graldiss was always on the lookout for any sign of behavior that might reveal a deviant tendency, but since he still came to take Agnar hunting he must not have found any. Now Talon was going to take Agnar to be with a whole lot of other dragons. He was nervous about how they would treat him.

"Just act naturally," Talon told him. "In a crowd you don't look any different than any other youngling. If you have any problems you can turn to Graldiss and Ittra."

"What about you? I would feel better if I could stay with you." Agnar leaned against Talon's chair.

"The last thing you need is to be identified with the only human who will be there. Take my advice and stick with Graldiss." Talon knew that he would have his own set of problems.

Talon was under no misconception that Ittra's endorsement, Magrid's essence and the support of his followers would carry him very far with the dragons of the other colonies. His best bet was not to *look* the part of a powerful wizard, keep it understated, don't look threatening or commanding. There was little chance of his blending in like Agnar could, but he might have to look to Graldiss for physical back up.

On the morning of the festival Talon used one of Olwin's old spells called Bag-o-Plenty and filled it with fifty large jars of marmalade, fifty giant loaves of bread and some wrapped packages. He polished Agnar's horn-buds and spines, scraped the dirt from under the sharp claws, and made sure all of Agnar's molting scales were picked off. Just after sunset Graldiss contacted Talon and the wizard transported himself and Agnar to his cavern in the mountain. He made contact with Ittra and waited.

There was no doubt when the Queen began to transport her colony to the festival. The mountain rang like a giant bell. The council members were the first to go, then elders and honored dragons. Ittra was moving groups of twenty dragons as quickly as they could gather in the hatching cave. She was not trying to compete with the other older queens to get her dragons to the festival grounds, but she didn't want to put them at a disadvantage by being late. Half-way through the process Ittra called Talon and his group to the hatching cave.

Talon was encircled protectively by his followers. Agnar was at his side. There was a tingle and darkness, just before the light returned the most perfect bell tone sounded. Talon was surprised by the warm breeze and fruit-scented air. Dragons of all shape, size and color could be seen in the blue sky above and on the lush green grass below. Before Talon's escort could move off of the landing field they were approached by a massive blue dragon. Talon sensed he had met her somewhere before. Magrid's memory shoved the name Py to Talon's lips. The circle of dragons parted and Talon dropped to his knees, his eyes lowered in submission, he held his arms wide to accept any fate the great Queen had for him.

By now a large number of dragons turned their attention to the strange scene being played out on the landing field. At the sight of a human an outraged roar filled the air. The area around and above the landing field became very crowded. A short low growl from the Queen silenced the dragons. A great claw reached out toward Talon's head. Talon sent a quiet word of farewell to Graldiss. He felt the weight of the foot bare down on his head, but he refused to have his face pushed into the dirt and stiffened to take the pressure. To his surprise, Talon felt the Queen's mind touch his. In a small, dark corner of Talon's mind Py found Magrid's memories and power.

"You are so young," the great Queen's voice filled his mind. "Why did my sister choose a child for the role of Krrig Daa?"

"I don't think it was her choice, Great Queen, anymore than it was mine," Talon answered.

"And would you give up this role if given the choice?" The Queen's voice was deceptively gentle when she asked the question.

Talon did not let a second lapse before he answered. "Never." But he felt she was expecting more. "Some days are more difficult than others, and I wish for a quiet place under the stars. But I can't escape from myself, can I? If I chose to live in a dark hole I would still be the Krrig Daa. I might be young, but I'm not immature, I'll face my destiny and accept it, not run and hide."

The heavy foot lifted from Talon's head. "Well said," the Queen said aloud. "Perhaps youth has its advantages. And you *are* wise above your years, you come in the guise of a simple man, not the powerful wizard I know you to be." In a voice loud enough for all to hear the mighty Queen proclaimed: "I welcome this boy-wizard. He has my sanction and that of every Queen here today. No harm will come to him."

Talon rose. He was grateful she had not mentioned that he was the Krrig Daa. One step at a time.

Py looked at Agnar, who knelt nervously. "Be at peace, youngling. The Queens have accepted the decision of our sister Ittra. We will not judge today whether your choice to live was brave or selfish, only time will tell." The Queen stepped back and took to the air.

Talon got to his feet feeling that he had just jumped a great hurdle. Minutes later Ittra's party arrived. Talon was surprised to see Graldiss carrying the Queen egg. The sour look on Manett's face spoke volumes. Talon allowed a grin to spread across his face. After Ittra joined the four within-egg queens under a gigantic tree, Graldiss joined Talon to hear about his meeting with Py.

"Impressive," Graldiss said. "What was it like?"

Talon shook his head. "I thought she was going to squish me like a pumpkin. Ittra must have talked to her, though. Queen Py knew to look for Magrid's memories and she knew about Agnar." Talon saw that the dragons from Ittra's colony had set up a type of camp around a stand of aspen trees. Assorted bags, wrapped packages, and covered pots were neatly organized under the shady branches. Talon put his bag with the others.

He stood for some time, amazed at the diversity of the beasts that filled the valley floor and dotted the sky. He had become used to the appearance of his own colony and had not considered that other dragons might look different. While his dragons were of a single color, all around him were striped and spotted beasts with brilliant colors and patterns.

He saw horns, curved spikes, elaborately frilled wings, and vicious-looking tails. With time he began to see similarities among members of the individual colonies and their Queens. It didn't take long for Talon to appreciate the simplicity of his own dragons. Some of the colonies were quite large; they must have been more successful than others in fighting off or hiding from attacking humans. Different colonies also varied in the size of their dragons. Some fully grown dragons were no larger than Agnar had been when he hatched; their younglings were closer in size to squirrels. Other dragons were tremendously large, almost ridiculously so, and were land-bound with only small decorative wings.

Agnar nipped at Talon's hand. "Are we going to stand here all morning? I want to go and play."

Talon smiled, he had forgotten that the youngling had had no contact with others his own age. "Well I don't know why you are still here, then. Go and have fun." He watched Agnar fly away with the apprehension of a new parent. With his own trepidation, Talon left the safety of his colony's grove of trees and joined the party. He followed his nose to the food area. The ground was covered with delicious dragon delicacies. A rather plump green dragon stood watch over the food. Talon put out his five large pots of sheep-eye marmalade and used a quick release of magic to slice and toast the large loaves of bread.

The dragons watched Talon warily. The word had quickly spread that this human, this wizard, was living with Ittra's colony. There were rumors that he was a dragon transformed into a human. Talon's followers must have begun to spread the word of Talon's true nature; because he was getting reverent glances. Py's sanction kept the dissenters quiet.

After the first hour of Talon's arrival, he was no longer seen as the enemy or a curiosity. He was allowed to join in the magic trials, where he put in a good showing. He was careful not to be too obvious about losing. He had gotten compliments on his marmalade and provided a good laugh when he discovered that the liver pie was of the uncooked variety.

As he moved around the other dragons he noticed that some of the decorations he had seen before were actually painted designs or fabric accessories. He learned dragons could be as vain about their appearance as humans. And if he closed his eyes he might imagine that this was a gathering of townsfolk during a summer fair. It was hard to imagine this species could be so hated by his own; the two were so much alike.

Talon kept an eye out for Agnar. Happily his fear of the youngling being ostracized by the others was unfounded. Though a few clutchmates stuck together, most of the younglings intermingled and they never considered that the blue dragon they chased through the tall grass was an outcast in his own colony. When Agnar showed off his light juggling he was a hit. He tried to teach his new friends how to create the floating lights, but learned that most of his fellow younglings had little or no knowledge of magic. Talon was thrilled to see some of their own colony included Agnar in their hunting games and chases. Perhaps the little dragon's future was not as grim as Talon had thought it would be.

A few hours later Talon made his way to the elaborately decorated Queen's Nest. He felt a golden chime of their conversations that silenced as he drew close. "I wondered when you would come and pay your respects," Ittra scolded

Talon bowed elaborately. "Please, mistress, forgive your humble servant."

There was a tinkle of laughter from the other eggs. "See what I have to put up with?" Ittra said with mock severity. "Humans! No respect."

Talon lovingly rubbed his Queen's egg. "Thank you for breaking the ice for me and Agnar."

"It was the least I could do. I didn't want your lifeless body on my conscience."

Talon stayed with the Queens for some time before they shooed him off to enjoy himself.

As the sun rose high into the sky many of the older dragons retreated to the shade of the trees. Talon sat off to the side, listening to the news of their colonies. Tollina spoke of the disaster of having their Queen stolen and the part Talon played in her retrieval. When asked about the rumors of dragons living with humans, Manett changed the subject. Talon remained silent; this was not the time for revolutionary ideas. Talon learned that some colonies were still at war with humans. Many elders counseled the total elimination of the humans, while many others were tired of the conflict and advised treaties rather than killings.

Talon stayed out of the debate. Instead, he watched the flying exhibitions. It was incredible that such large beasts were so agile in the air. The intricate swoops and dives, spins and curls looked like a dance. Some of the dragons wore colorful fabric streamers on their necks and tails; others wore bells or whistled as they made their complex aerial maneuvers. When Talon noticed a large number of dragons drifting just below the artistic flyers, he realized that these mid-air acrobats were *males* and their displays were for the benefit of *female* dragons. He smiled and looked away.

When the elders rose from their discussions to take part in other activities a few remained behind. The small, purple, horned dragon looked intently at Talon. “I have heard rumors, human.”

The large, blue-striped dragon nodded. "We would like to know the truth behind them."

Talon sighed and leaned back against a tree. "I don't know what you have heard, but I won't pretend not to know what you are talking about. The reason I am here, the reason Py did not kill me instantly is that I hold the memories and power of Queen Magrid." Talon waited until the shock sunk in. "She bestowed such an honor on me because she felt that I was special. It seems that I was born with the ability to perform magic, though I did not know it until later. After befriending a dragon, circumstances arose that made me shrink him in size to free him from an evil wizard. I apprenticed to Olwin of Carthis, who, it seems, knew that I was no ordinary young soldier. With no intention, I found myself being thrust into dragon prophecy. Magrid felt so strongly about my role as the Krrig Daa that when she died I was allowed to inherit her power." When the two dragons had time to take in this information Talon continued. "I've been living with Magrid's colony where I have been trying to bring humans and dragons together. I have also had the privilege of rescuing Queen Ittra when she was stolen by a human with evil intentions." Talon took a deep breath. "Are there any other rumors I haven't admitted to yet?"

The purple dragon laughed. "So much drama for one so young. I guess we can throw out the notion that you swallowed Magrid whole, or that you could extinguish the sun with a snap of your fingers."

It was Talon's turn to laugh. "I was warned by my friend Graldiss that it was unwise to play with nature."

The striped dragon rose and shook out her tail. "Magrid was a wise dragon, and a good Queen. She might have very well been right in her assessment of you, but the majority of us will not accept a human as the Krrig Daa. I will reserve judgment, if you don't mind." Talon shrugged. "But it does you credit to come here with humility rather than playing the part of a mighty wizard fulfilling dragon prophecy." She left the trees.

The small purple dragon studied Talon. "Don't worry about Teffia; she's skeptical about the sun rising in the morning. Being honest with her was the best course. She'll come around in a decade or two. Luckily her Queen is not so cynical. I'll take your story to my colony. If they choose to believe, someone will be sent to speak with you." The dragon took to the air.

"Pardon me, but I don't know your name," Talon called after her.

"Betto," she called back as she soared into the blue sky.

Down in the meadow, dragons were separating into groups. Spectators crowded around. Talon joined the onlookers. He overheard wagers being made against the skill of one contestant over another and came to the conclusion that these were the trials of dragon-skill. He scanned the competitors for members of his own colony. Throughout the afternoon Talon watched dragons large and small battle savagely to push each other out of a stone ring. Piles of logs were lit ablaze from varied distances by streams of belched flames. Hunters were timed and their prey weighed. Content was as important as detail when the air-painting was judged. Talon could not keep his eyes on the speed races; he saw that it was useless to run from any dragon. He laughed until his sides hurt when the eating contests took place; it would take hours to clean off the jellied faces. By nightfall Talon's voice was raw from cheering. His colony had made a good showing, placing in the top ten of five trials.

As the sun went down a huge bonfire was lit. Dragons drifted to the flames. Colonies intermingled, new friends sat together within the glowing light. Talon looked for Agnar, and found him chatting happily with five younglings of varied size.

"He's done very well today."

Talon turned to Graldiss. "It will be hard for him to return to a solitary life."

Graldiss shrugged. "I don't know that he will have to. He has shown himself to be a very amiable young dragon. He has made many friends in our own colony. I don't think he will be looked on as an outcast after today."

"I hope you're right." Talon sat next to Graldiss, leaning against the muscled thigh. "This has been an amazing day."

"It's not over yet." Talon looked quizzically at his friend. "There will be stories and singing well into the night."

"Nudge me if I start to doze off."

There was no chance at all for Talon to fall asleep. The plump dragon that had guarded the food all day transported what remained to an open area next to the fire. Bits and pieces of the food disappeared quickly. The animals that had been retrieved during the hunting trials were roasted slowly in the flames. Talon found it curious that the dragons would cook their meat. Graldiss had often eaten his prey raw after hunting it down.

"I don't see what's so curious about it," the dragon replied, "we do have a built in roaster. But some times we have to eat and run. A chance for a good barbeque is never passed up."

As the meat roasted and sputtered, a thin orange dragon stood before the fire and began to recite the story of how dragons brought mankind out of the mud and taught them the ways of magic. There were cheers and jeers but this was a story aimed only at retelling the event, not firing emotions, and no one even glanced in Talon's direction. When the story was over, another dragon rose. Talon couldn't see him from across the bonfire. This dragon recited the story of Gillidra the Mighty who lead his colony to victory against the Northern Pelia dragons. The battle was played out in great detail, descendants from both colonies called out names of their fallen ancestors. There was no spitefulness, or call for revenge. On into the night the stories of the dragons were told, some of them Talon knew from Magrid's memories. Fernley would have given anything to be there with paper and ink.

After consulting with Ittra, Talon climbed atop a large stump and raised his hand for attention. Since Ittra could not be at this gathering before the fire, Talon thought it was proper for him to tell a story from Magrid's memory. He told the story of the siege of Korinot.

"Two hundred and twenty eight years ago the army of the vicious King Telebiok," Talon spit into the fire, "laid siege to Mount Crinnelia. They attacked with horrible barbed arrows and long, thin spears of hot metal. Many valiant dragons fell in the twenty days of combat." Talon paused while the names of the fallen were shouted out. "On the twenty first day our dragons retreated into the caves to heal and plan a counter attack. But while they recovered Telebiok sealed the entrances to the caves and brought forth ten massive trebuchets to bombard the mountain. For twelve days our dragons endured.

Days and nights of the constant pounding of boulders were beginning to take their toll. Caverns and tunnels collapsed until only the hatching cave remained. Forty two dragons, young, old, and injured, huddled together, sure that their fate was to be buried within the mountain. But fate had other plans. On the thirteenth day a boulder struck the ceiling of the hatching cave and a small hole was created. At first there was only panic, they thought the end was near. But the young Queen saw opportunity, not tragedy." Magrid's name was shouted with pride. "The daring Queen was just small enough to fit through the new opening. She told her dragons to be brave, that she would return with help. She escaped the battered mountain when the night was at its darkest. Her colony tried to be brave, but hunger and the constant banging of boulders undermined their courage. When a week had gone by with no sign of their Queen, despair began to set in. The younglings were starving, everyone was weak from hunger. Their only hope of surviving was to share their own flesh to feed the younglings. Wings and tails were sacrificed for a few more days of life." Names were again shouted out. Talon noticed tears in eyes of many listeners. "Just when all seemed lost the weakened dragons noticed the boulders ceased to pound on their mountain. From inside the cave, sounds of a mighty battle could be heard. The young Queen flew through the now enlarged hole to tell her dragons of their approaching victory. She wept when she saw the condition of her colony. Magrid became so enraged that she stormed from the cave to avenge her colony. Hours later, when she returned to the hatching cave, bloody from battle, she carried the head of King Telebiok and lit it aflame before her colony." A tremendous cheer rose around the bonfire.

Talon stepped down and slumped to the ground. The memory of such a tragedy was almost too much for him. To his surprise, Talon was lifted into the air and passed from dragon to dragon until he arrived at the feet of Queen Py.

"Thank you for bringing this story back to us." The Queen wiped a tear from her cheek. "You have honored us with Magrid's memories." Talon wordlessly accepted the compliment. "Many here were not pleased to have you included in our celebration, but you have proven yourself worthy."

"It was I who was honored by a great Queen to bear her memories," Talon said solemnly. "And again I was honored to be allowed where no human has a right to be. In gratitude, I would like to offer you a burden I carry." Talon reached inside his shirt and drew out a pair of gold rings strung on a leather strap. A gasp of recognition spread around the fire. "For many decades men have hidden these Rings from those who would use them to destroy your race. I feel it is time that they are given to you." He held the Rings of Ko-Mon Po out to Py, who took them in her mighty claw. A cheer rose up, and Talon knew he had been right to give them to the Queen.

The small purple dragon Talon had spoken to earlier stepped up to Queen Py. The Queen bent down to allow her to speak privately. Py nodded and held up her wings to quiet the crowd. She turned again to Talon. "Queen Betto asks if you would honor her with an extended visiting to her colony."

The purple dragon bowed her head slightly. "I have consulted with Queen Ittra, who feels it would be as beneficial to you as it will be for us. Will you come with us?"

Talon didn't know what to say. He felt torn between this honor and his responsibilities with Agnar, the work he had started with his own colony, and the friends he had made.

Graldiss saw Talon's dilemma and spoke within his mind. "I will handle everything. Don't pass this up."

Talon smiled to his friend. He bowed to the Queens. "Thank you for the privilege you are bestowing on me. I don't feel worthy, but then I've always been the modest type." The two Queens laughed.

Talon rejoined his friend. "Interesting twist on the day," Graldiss said.

Talon could hear the pride in his voice. "I didn't expect anything like *this*."

"They'll expect you to go with them tonight. I'll bring your things in a few days."

Talon looked up at his friend. "What about Agnar? Will he feel that I'm deserting him? If he's not accepted by the others he'll be alone." Talon knew this would not be the case, but he couldn't think of any other objection to make.

"I'm sure Ittra will see that he's accepted, and I'll explain everything to him and watch over him like a big brother. Anything else?"

Talon wished he could talk this over with Ittra, it was happening so fast. But he couldn't deny the excitement that made him want to jump up and down like a youngling.

"Manett doesn't look happy about this," Graldiss said.

Talon looked over at the elder. He was surprised at the loathsome look on the dragon's face. "I would have thought she would be happy to be rid of me."

Graldiss looked down at Talon and grinned. "But don't you see, this validates everything about you that she hates. You are now more powerful than you were just as the Krrig Daa. Without knowing the destiny you hold, they accepted you...as a human."

Talon was speechless. He was glad the darkness hid his reddened cheeks.

When the full moon began to descend a frilled dragon sang out a single note. The note grew in strength as thousands of dragons joined in. A second, third and fourth note filled out the harmony until every dragon's voice was raised in beautiful song. Talon longed to join in, but his voice was too weak.

"Use your flute, silly," Ittra said from the Queen's Nest.

Talon drew his flute from his pocket and raised it to his lips. He closed his eyes and listened to the wordless singing of the dragons, letting it fill his very soul. Without thinking Talon began to play. His innate magic brought forth a dramatic melody. The dragons were stunned by such depth of feeling. They shifted their own song to compliment Talon's playing until the glorious music brought tears to their eyes. Only one dragon did not raise her voice to accompany Talon. But no one paid the least attention to her.

When Talon brought his song to a close and opened his eyes he was confused by the sudden silence. He thought he must have done something wrong in playing along. He started to turn away in embarrassment, and when the dragons roared, he considered transporting himself far away. But the dragons didn't look angry; they didn't look like they were going to attack. Talon turned to Graldiss to see what he should do. The grin on the dragon's face was reassuring.

"More!" the dragons shouted.

Py's voice spoke to Talon: "Lead us in song, Krrig Daa."

Talon's face beamed with pride. He lifted the flute. Thousands of faces turned to him, waiting. Talon closed his eyes and played.

The End

Diana spent her childhood in the lush green Willamette Valley of Oregon. She knew there had to be dragons hidden in the forests. Diana studied History at Oregon State University with the intention of writing historical romance novels. In 1992 the Metz family moved to Rock Springs, Wyoming, where there are very few trees and only small dragons. Diana started writing stories for her three children in 1997.